THE LAST BUTTERFLY

Most of the facts in this story are true. Terezin was a concentration camp sixty miles from Prague, wherein were collected some of the greatest talents in Europe. Many of them taught (unofficially) and entertained the children. Among them was the hero of this story.

Of the 140,000 people who passed through Terezin on their way to Auschwitz, only 1300 are known to have survived. Of the 1500 children who knew Terezin, a few more than 100 are alive.

The Last Butterfly

MICHAEL JACOT

NEW ENGLISH LIBRARY
TIMES MIRROR

First published in Great Britain by New English Library, 1974
© 1973 by Michael Jacot

*

FIRST NEL PAPERBACK EDITION OCTOBER 1975

*

NEL Books are published by
New English Library Limited from Barnard's Inn, Holborn, London, E.C.1.
Made and printed in Great Britain by Hunt Barnard Printing Ltd., Aylesbury, Bucks.

45002447 4

The poem, 'The Butterfly', used in the novel, was written by Pavel Friedmann. He went to the gas chamber at Auschwitz, September 29, 1944. The poem is taken from *I Never Saw Another Butterfly*, edited by M. Volavkova, 1964. McGraw-Hill Book Company. Used with permission of the McGraw-Hill Book Company.

The author wishes to acknowledge gratefully the Jewish Museum, Prague, for their co-operation and assistance.

In the interests of readability, the author has anglicised many Czech and Slovak names and words, leaving off accents. He apologises to Czech-speaking readers.

There once lived a king who hated butchers. So he had every butcher in the kingdom put to death.

Then he began to hate all cyclists, and he started a program to exterminate them all too.

Someone asked, 'Why cyclists?'

To which he replied, 'For the same reason as butchers.'

The theme of a play written by the inmates of Terezin.

To all my family

1

The evening had slipped into night without Antonin even noticing it. He stood at the window of his room in the musty old Hotel Majestic and peered through the hole his breath had made on the frosted glass.

Freshly-powdered snow covered most of the cobble-stones in the town square. A curtain of cloud draped itself over the faint November moon. It was a depressing sight. And Antonin was already depressed.

Centuries of dank farm air had given most of the Baroque buildings around the square a certain shapeless monotony. The church, for all its gilt and ormolu, visibly bore the war scars which three years without repair had left. The statue to St Stanislaus, at the church doors, added the final touch of decay with its peeling gold paint.

At its base someone had chalked a swastika. Underneath in childish hand Antonin saw the word: HITLER. And under it a crude drawing of a pig.

A few people were already at the theatre entrance opposite, brushing back the blackout curtain as they went in.

On that side of the square the snow had been worn away by the feet of passing farmers. The cobble-stones glistened with slippery wetness.

On the south side of the square, outside the German officers' mess, the snow still lay undisturbed. No one had ventured across the pavement. A small detour of foot prints suggested local contempt for the building.

Antonin drew the blackout curtain across his window and turned on the electric light. He sat on the edge of the bed. He shivered. The damp air in the room seeped into the very marrow of his bones.

'It's not only me, it's the whole bloody country,' he said out loud.

Czechoslovakia was living in a padded grey silence.

'They expect you to go out on to that stage and wipe out the whole depressing world from their minds . . . and make them laugh.'

Antonin raised himself enough to reach the butt of a cigarette that lay in the glass ashtray beside the dressing table mirror.

'I'll smoke it now,' he said, 'to hell with saving it until after the show. Perhaps Ales will give me a cigar.'

He stuck the butt on the end of a pin. He could already feel the taste of it in his mouth. The match flared weakly at the third strike. Time for two puffs only, then he must make his way to the theatre.

'Jesus-Maria! If only I didn't feel so goddamn tired!'

The cigarette made him cough, but he kept it between his lips.

'It's not just me, it's everyone!' he repeated.

The thought was razor sharp, and too painful for him to realise that the cigarette was actually burning his top lip.

The mask! It was getting more and more difficult to put it on. Especially when you felt so tired. When you tried to do it, it knotted your stomach and brought bile to your mouth. But people expected it. They expected to see you as they imagined you to be.

Putting the mask on was something his father had taught him years ago. You started with your toes, tautening the muscles, stiffening your calves, throwing your hips forward and straightening your shoulders. Finally you worked on your face, racking your brain into place for the quick response, the cocky, devil-may-care, eager, bloody smile! At one time he could manage it almost instantaneously.

'Sir!'

A boy of sixteen or so stood before him. Antonin stopped in his path. The boy was smiling. He held out something in his hand. Antonin noticed that the wet, ragged edge of the boy's coat sleeve had chapped his wrists.

The package was wrapped in newspaper. The boy's face reddened.

'Mr Antonin . . . my father asked me to bring you this.'

Antonin was struggling for the mask.

'Sir, it's for you . . . from my father,' the boy repeated.

'Thank you . . . and thank your father,' Antonin managed to say.

The boy disappeared. Antonin unwrapped the newspaper. There was a sausage and some boiled potatoes. And a note: 'From an admirer.' It was written in a crude farm hand.

Antonin smiled. He reached out for the stage door handle and firmly pulled it towards him. The mask!

The green room at the Town Theatre always reminded Antonin of a big farmhouse kitchen. Its faded yellow walls and high ceiling gave it a utilitarian air, which the old theatre bills and portraits of past stars failed to disperse.

In the centre of the room was a huge, long, oak table. In one corner a primus stove stood on a large trunk. Tonight, a kettle gently simmered on it. In the other corner a square, black, wood-fired stove heated the room. Benches with make-up mirrors attached to them lined the walls.

The air was filled with a mixture of cigar smoke, sour, black bread, stale sausage and make-up. It was not an unpleasant smell to Antonin. The first twitch of it in his nostrils as he opened the door had a great deal of meaning for him. At forty, he could not even remember the first time he had smelt it. It had been a part of his father when he was helping him with his act as a small boy. He always sniffed at it a few times before focusing on the room. It was like an animal. This was his nest.

Tonight, Olga Prokes, the singer, sat at the foot of the table in her tight, red Spanish costume, smoothing out the wrinkles under her eyes with make-up. The dwarfs, Heinrich and Dagmar, their chins barely in view over the oak table, shared a sausage. The juggler, Stepanek, sat half hidden behind a bottle of wine, and the male falsetto, Rudi Kvasnicka, aimlessly filed his nails, occasionally tossing back his rich black hair with a dainty flick of the head.

Jiri Ales was doing what he always did. He was walking up and down, an unlit cigar in his mouth, humming. His hands behind his back, he strutted about like a cock. Ales was a grey-haired, tight-lipped man who wore down his shoe leather throughout every performance since he had been appointed theatre manager.

Antonin stepped into the circle of light.

'*Dobry vecer*,' he said and shook hands with Stepanek who was already almost drunk enough to perform his juggling. Nodding at Olga and at others round the table, he sat down.

An automatic chorus of '*Dobry vecer*' greeted him. A smile from the dwarfed Dagmar. This was his chair. He was entitled to it. Like an abbot in a monastery. In a moment he would go to the men's lavatory to change into baggy trousers and a green velvet jacket. But for now it was his chair. He occupied it as some men occupy an officer's uniform.

Instinctively, despite the fact his wife, Anna, had been dead for nearly a year now, he reached out to where she usually put his coffee cup. He withdrew his hand quickly with a slight, embarrassed smile; but not fast enough. He caught Rudi's lips tightening into a grin.

Through the thick walls they could hear the audience clapping. The dog act was over. Olga rose and put out her cigarette. She cleared her throat. Antonin winked at her. His sign of good luck.

The door slammed and her perfume lingered in the stale air beside Antonin.

'For Christ's sake, can't you stand still?' he yelled at Ales.

'So all right, all right.'

'What's up anyway? The house is full and we're sold out all week. It says so outside!'

'Nothing's up.'

Ales stopped suddenly beside Antonin.

'Are you going to drop that "milking" routine . . . like we said, Antonin?'

'I'm dropping nothing.'

Ales started to move again.

'Might be an idea, Antonin. In Prague last week I heard some jokes from this new guy . . . what's his name? . . . Robicek?'

'Jan Robicek?'

'At the Lucerna.'

'He stole them from his father . . . who stole them from my father. . . . '

'No. This is new stuff. There was one about a man who fell under a car and . . . '

Antonin stood up and tilted his head to one side mimicking Ales. Then he strutted up and down the other side of the table in time with him.

'I'm only asking you to try . . . '

'I'm only asking you to try . . . ' Antonin aped.

Ales never looked at him. Rudi had finished his nails and was blowing on them.

'You'd better get dressed. We'll talk later,' said Ales.

'Talk later. Talk later,' mimicked Antonin. Rudi laughed

and the dwarfs were laughing too. Antonin locked his knuckles together on his chest, stood on tip-toe and let the folds of his face droop in sadness. The dwarfs laughed again.

Antonin rose with his wardrobe to change in the lavatory. As he closed the door he was glad that he could not hear what was said after he left. He busied his mind with thoughts about his act. He always did two spots in each show. He ended each half. He was on next.

2

Olga made a big finish. It wasn't exactly in keeping with her Spanish costume, but it was big – an aria from *Brünnehilde*. Her voice crashed against the five tiny balconies in the Town Theatre and came back at her like thunder.

Through the back-drop Antonin could see her arms rise to clasp the whole farm audience to her ample bosom and then fall dramatically as the note hit the heights.

A fair applause greeted her. Antonin wondered if he dare start off mimicking that. He laughed inwardly. I'd better not. I'm in enough trouble with Ales. Another goddamn row and he'll kill me . . . or I'll kill him!

The band was *oom-paa-paaing* its way through his intro – a heavy rendition of the overture from *The Barber of Seville*.

The curtain was spinning up to the flies and he was on, centre stage, with the big amber spot on him.

He stood for a second, after the music and clapping had died, his hands clasped characteristically on his stomach and his shoulders sagging. His head seemed to tilt sadly to the right, his chin to rest on his chest.

He was shaking inside. Really shaking.

He lifted his eyes slowly, coming to life like a flower. The rows and rows of red faces, well fed, despite the war, and blossoming like raw meat in the dim light, made him shake even more.

He could, in that split second before he spoke, distinguish children, toothless grandmothers and unshaven middle-aged men.

'I've got to make them laugh. You are bloody well going to laugh,' he said to himself.

Suddenly, automatically, as he had done for thirty years, his body stiffened and his hands fell lightly and naturally into his pockets.

'I'm walking down the street and this bum comes up to me

and says "Mister, I haven't had a bite to eat in three days." So I bit him.'

He heard a titter of attention. One man was wiping his face on his handkerchief. A child was whispering to his mother. An old man was coughing.

Antonin took his usual place down stage. The amber spot followed. He could even smell them from here, near the edge of the stage.

He wondered if the shaking was noticeable.

'This man asked his doctor, "Will I be able to play the piano after my operation?" "Sure," the doctor said, and the man says, "Funny, I couldn't do it before." '

There was a bigger laugh this time. Obviously jokes were not what they wanted. He wished to Christ he knew what it was they were after.

'Thank you. Thank you. And now for the funny part!'

His body became a sack. He fell like a heap of crumpled clothing on the stage.

As he lay there for a second listening to the laughter, he could smell the oak boards, powdered with talcum from the dancing act.

He jumped up. By now his stomach was in a knot and his wrists were swollen from the pressure of trying.

He decided to put one of his old routines back into the act. He raised his head, buttoned up his green jacket and walked along with strutting gait. He was the farmer visiting Prague. Wenceslaus Square. The band recognised it and struck up some Saturday evening music.

An imaginary stick was in Antonin's right hand and on his left arm a lady whom he had just met in the street. Anyone could see she was a lady because Antonin's left side seemed to mince along as part of her.

In mime he made the motions of dancing together and then, by putting his hands to the side of his face, of sleep. A double take at the audience brought a laugh.

An imaginary hand went into Antonin's breast pocket. His eyebrows raised. He pretended to be tickled. Then in a delayed reaction he saw his own wallet being opened and money being taken from it.

His face once again went to the audience in shock. More laughter. The old man was still wiping his face with his handkerchief. Somewhere, up in the third balcony, a child shouted, 'She's taken his wallet!'

Antonin swung round to the woman he'd picked up and gave chase round the stage.

Then he turned on one foot and faced the audience again. There was a spontaneous round of applause. But it was not enough. Antonin's legs began to shake.

He held up his hands to stop the applause, but it had already faded to nothing.

He gestured with his arms that there was a shop with fresh bread in it. He rubbed his stomach in hunger, and became small and lonely. But by now all he wanted to do was to get off. He still had another spot to do tonight. He had to come on again to finish the show and the thought stuck like a piece of apple in a hollow tooth.

Mechanically he went through the motions of trying to distract the shopkeeper's attention so that he could steal a loaf. The 'fly on the counter' routine . . . he followed the fly with his eyes almost out into the audience and then smacked it . . . without killing it. He turned suddenly and grabbed the bread . . . too late. The shopkeeper saw him and whistled for the police. He was taken away.

This routine ended his act for the first half. It was a famous bit. Too famous. Too well known to the old in the audience and too incomprehensible for the very young.

He drew out a very long checkered handkerchief and wiped his brow. He was beaten. Absolutely beaten. But he could not show it. It was all he could do to get off the stage. The curtain fell quickly.

3

Jiri Ales was in the green room. He was alone. The rest of the cast had gone to the bar for the interval. Ales was still walking.

Antonin reached under the table for his coat pocket and pulled out the sausage and cold potato. He took a penknife from his pocket and sliced the sausage slowly. With the end of the knife he put two slices in his mouth and then bit into the potato.

When he looked up Ales was holding out a cup of coffee for him.

'Where's everyone?'

'At the bar.'

Antonin sensed that Ales had sent them there so that he could talk to him alone.

'Antonin . . . ' Ales cleared his throat. 'How were they?'

'What you'd expect. From old women and kids. But I think I've got the secret. I'm going to add something for the second spot. You see, I've got them in the mood now. . . .'

'What are you going to add?'

'You'll see.'

'Antonin . . . may I suggest something . . . ?'

Antonin took a bit of sausage. He held up the other end for Ales. Might as well make a friend. . . .

'No charge,' he said, 'that is unless you've got a cigarette?'

Ales withdrew one from his trouser pocket and handed it over. He declined the sausage.

'Now for God's sake, stop walking up and down.'

'Antonin, go to Prague. Take a few weeks off. I'll have you back . . . I promise . . . but you must get some rest and . . . listen to Robicek . . . he's good . . . there's another guy . . . I forget his name, but he's a big hit at the night clubs . . . satire and stuff. . . . '

Ales's face was only a few inches away. He was leaning on the table and his fat knuckles were white. Antonin looked

17

slowly into his face. The mask, he prayed, send me my mask. But there was no energy left to summon it.

'Jesus-Maria, leave me alone,' he said slowly, facing Ales.

Antonin never remembered how long they sat together in the green room that night. But Ales did sit down and he did finish the sausage. Neither spoke. Even after the second half had started.

But Antonin knew then. And what was worse he knew that Ales knew too.

He remembered the green room door opening and a lot of laughter as some of the cast came in. He remembered the laughter dying gradually, like water from a badly turned off tap. The half empty coffee cup was between Antonin's hands. He tapped it back and forth, his eyes fixed on it, but seeing nothing. His lips were moving, but no words were coming out.

Antonin realised that it was the middle of the second half of the show before he pulled himself together.

He sat up proudly and looked around.

'I once met a Russian in a bar,' he said. 'Next to the Irish they are the most illogical people in the world. This man said, "I'm leaving now. If I'm not here tomorrow, I'll be here for three days!"'

He laughed. So did the people who had sat silently around him. The door burst open and Ondracek, the dog trainer, came in. Olga was on stage. He closed the door.

'Hey, I've something to tell you.'

Everyone turned to him with relief.

'Watch,' said Ondracek. He gave the Nazi salute.

Everyone, even Antonin, looked at him in astonishment.

'That's how high my dog can jump!' said Ondracek.

Ales laughed until the tears ran down his face. The dwarfs gave high pitched giggles.

'Hey, Antonin, sir, you're on!' It was the stage manager pushing his head round the door.

In a daze Antonin walked to the door. He could feel the eyes on him. He closed the door and waited. He breathed deeply. What was it his father used to say? 'If you're not ready, let them wait for you. They'll love you for it.'

That night Antonin never remembered the curtain going up. He was a puppet, doing a routine that was etched indelibly in his brain.

He reached the end of the act in a nightmare and was almost too overwhelmed to take his bow . . . it was an overbearing

18

moment as in a half sleep. But it was lucky. Because in the middle of the bow, his hair fell over his forehead, and when he straightened up, the hair had placed itself like a dark shadow just over one eye. His body slumped slightly. The mask. The mask! When he stood up again he was Hitler.

The reaction from the audience was slow, but when it came it was mingled with fear.

With his left finger posed as a toothbrush moustache, Antonin broke the hushed silence of the theatre by raising his right arm in the Nazi salute.

He paused . . . not too long, but for that second which years of timing had taught him. Then he said,

'That's how high my dog can jump!'

For a moment there was dead silence. Then it broke. Wave after wave of laughter and applause, a dam that had burst itself. It flooded Antonin. He bowed quickly and they were still calling for him to do an encore when he walked into the wings. Ales was there. His face was a sheet.

'You fool. You'll get us all arrested.'

Antonin hardly heard him.

In the green room he had already packed his trousers and jacket in his suitcase when Ales came in.

'What are you doing?'

'Leaving you and this goddamn circuit. I'm finished with you.'

'Listen, Antonin,' Ales was pleading now . . . 'what I said earlier on . . . I mean . . . come and have a drink and we'll talk about it. . . . '

'It's what you've wanted, isn't it?' Antonin snapped the case shut. 'Well, isn't it?'

'I . . . never . . . well, yes. Yes! Do you realise what you did? They'll close the theatre.'

'To hell with you and your bloody theatre. There's work in Prague. There people will understand. So . . . I'm going.'

He walked out.

As he left the hotel later that night to catch the milk train to Prague, Antonin felt the chill of the night as much as the stillness in the square.

The moon was high in the heavens now. The clouds had gone and the shadows were long and greenish. He walked slowly, shoulders bent, not caring much about the mask.

The station was half a mile to the south. After he had

19

crossed the square, the place was as still and silent as it had been before he entered it. The only change was the fresh row of footprints he'd left as he passed on the pavement outside the German officers' mess. The only footprints there.

4

It was very early. Thick grey mist swirled down from the hills surrounding Prague and settled twisting around the granite spires. Antonin, his coat turned up against the chill, made his way through the crowds in the Praha-Hlavni station. People were knocking against him as he pulled the heavy case after him. Many of the people were peasants coming into the city with bundles of food-stuffs. A soldier on crutches stood in the dim light of the main doors trying to light a cigarette.

Policemen in 'Protectorate' uniforms marched in pairs.

Antonin joined the groups of people trudging the snow-ridden streets.

There were no buses and the trams ran infrequently. Antonin walked slowly up Hybernska, past the town hall in Staromastske, and down Maislova Street.

It was much closer to the river here and the mists were thicker. Three old men, with the yellow Star of David on their coarse coats came towards him. They stopped talking and stood still as he passed them.

'*Dobry den,*' he shouted.

They did not reply.

There was no one else on the street, but Antonin had the feeling he was being watched from behind the blackout curtains.

At the end of the street he turned right. The building which housed his apartment was across the street. He looked up to the third floor. His blackouts were still in place.

His apartment was small, one large room with a kitchen and bathroom off to one side. He had lived in it since he and Anna were first married.

He kicked aside the mail which had been pushed under the door and opened the blackouts.

A photograph of Anna hung on the wall above the place where he put his suitcase. The black ribbon across one corner was dusty. Antonin brushed it clean with his sleeve.

Before sitting down he made a tour of the room, like a dog making sure its favourite basket hasn't been touched. He picked up a few ornaments on the mantelpiece, straightened a cushion on the overstuffed sofa and turned on the radio. The sign, in crude printed lettering, which it was obligatory to have on each radio, read: LISTENING TO AN ENEMY BROADCAST MEANS CAPITAL PUNISHMENT.

Antonin went to the huge mahogany wardrobe beside his bed and took out a bottle of wine. He poured himself a large glass and sat down. At one end of the sofa was a small chest of drawers. From the top drawer he took out a scrap book. As he flicked through the faded pages, he tried to make up his mind.

He snapped the book shut, opened it again, smiled as he recalled some dim memory, and half stood looking across at the telephone on its chromium hooks. He took more wine, looked at himself in the mirror above the mantelpiece, and straightened a few more objects. Then slowly he sat down; any excuse was better than making the call. Finally the book fell open on his knees. It so happened that it was at a page which was marked with a folded theatre bill. The bill was dated September 15, 1923. It listed all acts appearing at the National Theatre, Bratislava. His name was in big print at the top. It was the first time he had starred.

After that it had been easy for him until the war. He became known on the country circuit and loved, so that people would come up to him in the street and shake his hand.

Things had always been different in Prague. Louis, his agent, had tried him twice at Lucerna, but somehow he had never clicked.

Maybe today was the day that Prague was waiting for him. Hope came quickly to Antonin. He knew that it died quickly too.

He sprang up and went over to the telephone. Not yet used to the new dialing system which had been installed just at the beginning of the war, his fingers stumbled. Finally he heard the telephone ring at the other end.

'*Dobry den, Je to* . . . Louis? This is Antonin. Antonin Karas. . . .'

'When did you get back in town? I thought you were booked for the tour.'

'I'm taking a short rest. I got a bit run down and I'm going to start looking for something different. . . .'

'Good,' Louis's voice had a hollow ring to it.

Antonin decided to try to warm him up.

'I've got a lot of new material. I'd like to come and see you ... well, as soon as possible.'

'Things are slow here, Antonin. What with the blackout and the curfew, it's tough keeping a theatre open. ...'

'I've been thinking about that too. Could you make it on Monday, Louis?'

'Tuesday, perhaps, but I don't want you to think....'

'Tuesday at say ... two?'

'Yes, two. Why didn't you stay on the farm tour?'

'I got fed up with the lousy tour.'

'At least you were working.'

'I'll see you at two then. *Na shledanou.*'

Antonin put the receiver down quickly. He took down the rest of his wine.

Louis hadn't turned him down. He poured another glass of wine. He looked at himself in the mirror again, snatched up his coat and hat and left the apartment. Antonin needed bread, cheese and some potatoes. He took his battered ration card from his pocket and went into the street.

5

The Taverna Divadlo was a small café set under the arches of a fifteenth century monastery cellar. On its walls were draped rich velvet embroidered coats of arms of theatres. In previous times Prague theatres had been patronised by the rich.

Each table was lit by a stem of three candles and hence, despite the war, the Taverna Divadlo never suffered the power cuts like other cafés. It was too cold, of course, and its entrance was cluttered with sandbags. But if enough theatre people came in after the play, it was quite warm.

The taverna had one other advantage. The Nazis had not yet found it, and it remained free of soldiers. One could, if one really wanted to, Antonin thought as he waited for his friends Karel and Petr, pretend the war had not started.

It had one other advantage as far as Antonin was concerned. The proprietor and the patrons all knew him.

Antonin had been there all afternoon and the vapours from the wine were beginning to affect his head.

He could see Petr and Karel now, over the top of his wine glass, Karel looked thinner and more rubber-faced than ever. Petr waved at him. Petr, Antonin had known from the day he came into the theatre at Ostrava, fresh from the circus. He still looked like a circus clown. Even in his street clothes you couldn't mistake him. Everything was too small, except his shoes which unless you looked closely seemed to be worn on the wrong feet.

As they made their way to his table they were greeted by others. As was the custom they had to stop, shake hands, and pass the time of day with each person. It was an unwritten law. It bound them all together at a time when the rest of the world was crumbling.

Finally they reached his table. Petr embraced him first.

'Why didn't you tell us you were back? . . . A whole month, you say!'

'I needed time to think.' Karel was embracing him clumsily now.

They sat like long lost schoolboys at his table as he poured them some wine.

'*Na zdravi!*' they all toasted.

'They have me working in the trenches . . . ' said Karel.

'Jesus-Maria.' Antonin was trying to pull his wits together.

'It's not so bad,' said Karel. 'And I've lots of friends with me. It can't last forever.'

'I shouldn't be too sure,' said Antonin, 'all along the railway line they are building fortifications. . . . '

'Who are?'

'Jewish labour gangs. God knows where they come from.'

'They're taking them in lorries from Terezin,' said Petr.

Antonin's uncle had been taken to Terezin. He knew Terezin was a concentration camp about sixty kilometres from Prague, which had been set up by Hitler as a Jewish state, and according to reports over 60,000 Jews were interned there. Antonin wondered why Petr had mentioned the place. Was he trying to warn him?

'They haven't questioned you *yet*?' said Karel.

Antonin shook his head. 'There's no stamp on my identity card. Only my mother was Jewish.'

'You shouldn't have come back to Prague!'

'If they try to take me, they'll get more than they bargained for,' said Antonin, but his heart wasn't in it. There *was* something behind Petr's remarks.

'For Jesus' sake, let's talk about something else,' he said.

He pulled out a home-made cigarette and shared it with them.

'You two interested in an idea I have?' he asked. 'I've got something worked out . . . a plan. . . . '

'Yes?' Petr was sipping his wine.

'That empty theatre beside the Loreta convent. . . . '

'The Kabaret?' said Karel.

'As soon as it's all over, I'm going to buy it.'

'So you have a fortune stashed away?' said Petr.

'I've some cash, and that land around my cottage could bring a couple of thousand crowns. We'll do comedy. A truly comic theatre. They'll come in busloads from all over the country.'

'New material? New plays? New routines?' Karel shook his finger under Antonin's nose. 'Where'll you get 'em?'

'I've got that figured out too. People are ill now. The war has made them ill. They laugh at sick jokes with hidden political meanings. . . . '

'Like the Nazi salute?' said Petr.

There was a slight pause. So that was it! Petr *was* warning him.

'You heard about it?'

'It's all over town.'

'Don't worry! So what can they do to you?' said Karel.

Antonin finished his wine quickly and ordered another bottle.

'Of course! Why should they bother with someone like me!'

There was a pause.

'. . . and besides I'm serious about this theatre.'

'Why get so worked up now? The war's not over!'

'Because we have to prepare . . . be ready . . . it's our last chance. Don't you see?'

For a split second, Antonin caught the look on both of his friends' faces.

'Speaking for us two, it's a bit late now Toni,' said Karel.

'Well, it's not for me. I'm going to start again . . . right now. And I'm not going to let any bloody war stop me!'

'So, okay, good. Then let's talk it over,' said Petr. 'But I should warn you, it would have been better to stay in the country. But it's your life. So speak up – we'll listen.'

They listened. It was very late when Antonin left the café. Well after curfew. And Antonin was very drunk.

6

'What the hell . . . ?'

Antonin tried to free himself from the firm grip the youth
had on his arm. He had turned the corner from the café
trying to stay in the shadows.

'It's all right. I was waiting for you to come out. I'll see you
home . . . ' said the youth.

Antonin's eyes were focusing better now. He could see the
Star of David on the boy's sweater.

'Get the hell away from me. D'you want to get us both
arrested?'

'I'll have you home in two minutes.'

The boy began taking short cuts. At first Antonin tugged
to free his arm, but soon he gave up. He reluctantly allowed
himself to be dragged along like a puppy on a chain.

It was true. The boy took him home and in no time flat.
Antonin never remembered going up the stairs to the third
floor, and when he came to later, he was sleeping in his arm-
chair and the boy was sitting opposite on the sofa.

'You've been sleeping nearly an hour,' the boy had an
infectious grin. 'You'd like some coffee?'

'Real kava?'

'The real thing.' The boy handed Antonin a mug. 'I took
the liberty of making it in your kitchen.'

Antonin could smell it now. He let his nostrils take it in
slowly.

'But where did you get it?'

'I stole it from the officers' mess in Cinska Street.'

'You'll get yourself shot.'

'I doubt it. They're such fools. Our labour group has the
job of picking up the garbage there. The quartermaster has
itemised everything in the kitchens and the inventory is in
triplicate. Every item is then placed in an appropriate tin.
They're the same tins that the biscuits come in. Naturally

when new biscuits arrive we have the extra tins to throw away. We label them as we wish . . . flour, coffee, sugar, salt, etc. . . . then we swap tins. It's one hell of a laugh.'

'They'll find out. You must stop.'

'As long as the inventory is in triplicate and stamped with the date every month, they think everything is in order. Anyway that's not what I came to talk about. . . . My father was Cherniak.'

Antonin nodded slowly. 'Now I see the resemblance.'

'He often spoke about you. When they took him away on the Transport, I was thrown out of theatre school and I've been living on my wits ever since.'

'Did you ever hear from him?'

'No, but they told me he died.' The boy glanced down to his hands. Then up again to Antonin's face. 'My name is Pavel. I need your advice.'

'How can I refuse?' said Antonin, burying his nose in the coffee mug.

'I thought if you introduced me to Ales or someone, I might get a job on the country circuit. I know all my father's routines and some I've got up myself. . . . '

'Not with that on your papers . . . ' said Antonin, pointing to the Star of David.

'I've got forged papers.'

The boy produced them and Antonin looked them over.

'Cost you a fortune, eh?'

'I stole them. A friend put my picture on.'

'Stole? You are playing close to the bone, Pavel.'

'On the country circuit I could hide away until it's over.'

'What if Ales doesn't like your act?'

'I'll take anything. I'll sweep the stage. I'll at least be free.'

'That's funny. I left the circuit last month because I wanted to be free. I'll write you the letter anyway. There isn't a place on the circuit where my name isn't good for a job. . . . '

'I know. . . . '

'There's a pen and some ink in that drawer. The paper should be there too. Yes, my name's good,' he repeated, 'I've kept it that way and it's worth remembering . . . Pavel.'

The boy was standing over him with the pen in his hand.

Antonin's eyes were still blurry from the wine.

'A good name is the most important asset. If people don't respect you, you'll never make it.'

'I'll remember that.'

28

Antonin started to scribble a letter to Ales.

'And after the thing's over . . . come and see me. I'm open-ing a new theatre here. You'll read about it in the press. It's a secret, but it's all signed and sealed. It's going to be big . . . so come and see me.'

As Antonin finished he pulled out some cash and handed it to the boy with the letter.

'No, thank you, I really don't need it.'

'Take it, Pavel.'

Antonin drunkenly forced the money on him.

Pavel smiled nervously and put it in his pocket.

'You never know,' Antonin said, 'some day you may have to do me a favour.'

When the boy was gone, Antonin sat back in his chair and waited. It would soon be dawn. Soon after that people would start going to work. And soon after that the phone might ring.

But by ten o'clock it hadn't rung. Just as it hadn't rung every morning since Antonin had last been to see Louis. With a sudden jump from his chair in an effort to pull himself out of his depression, Antonin put on his coat and hat and decided to leave the phone unanswered.

But even as he went down the stairs to the street he thought he could hear it ring and was tempted to run up to answer it. When he stopped to make sure, it was only a ringing in his ears.

The sun was out and the air was crisp. He turned down Maislova to the old Jewish cemetery. Old people were standing sunning themselves on the pavement under the high wall of the cemetery.

Antonin always liked to walk in the cemetery. Apart from the feeling of history among the thousands of tightly cluttered tombstones there was peace there. It was over a thousand years old. The graves were often so old that the tombs had been worn away to smooth stones a few inches above the soil. The great oaks and poplars filtered the cool winter sun, and the little stone benches were set in such a manner that you could still be alone even though the cemetery was one of the favourite walking places in the area. As a matter of fact it was the only place where the few remaining Jewish children were allowed to play.

Today was no exception. Several little groups of children, under the wary eyes of black-clad mothers, ran among the ruined tombstones playing quietly.

Antonin had never considered himself Jewish. In fact he had never considered himself anything else but Czech. But today, surrounded by so many Jewish children, his Jewishness came alive. What did they do without their fathers and mothers? How did it feel to see your relatives taken away on a Transport? How could someone go on living a comparatively normal existence with fear and uncertainty as constant companions? The more he tried to brush away these thoughts, the more they came back.

Antonin fell into a sort of reverie. When he came to life again he was standing beside a group of five or six small children. They were silently watching him with big, fearful eyes.

It took a second or two for him to realise why they were afraid. He had no Star of David on his coat. A figure without one was a figure of fear.

Antonin smiled and took his hat off. As he put it back on his head, a gust of wind blew it off. One of the children giggled. The incident triggered something. He started to perform.

The wind came up again and he pulled his hat on to his head tightly with both hands. He rolled his eyes up to see the brim. Then he let go of the hat with both hands. The hat flew into the air, triggered by his thumbs. He jumped up for it and it flew ahead of him over the top of a tombstone. He vaulted the stone in pursuit. He caught it only to have it fly back over his head into the middle of the children. Arching his body back like a snake he caught with his left hand. The hat jumped again six feet into the air.

'It's alive,' said a small girl with blonde hair and pigtails.

They were laughing now. The fear had been forgotten.

Antonin flicked the hat ahead of him and it fell on to the head of a boy, covering his yamaka. Antonin fell in an attempt to reach it.

He could see, as he hit the ground, that the children were doubled over with laughter and clapping their hands in joy. He whipped himself up again and snatched the hat which soared into the air through the branches of the trees.

'Look out. It may hit you as it comes down,' he shouted. He waved with his arms for the children to scatter.

'It's alive. I tell you the hat's alive,' the pig-tailed girl screamed.

'It does this every Tuesday at this time,' said Antonin, taking the hat firmly between his two hands and pretending to force it into the ground. He held it there for a second.

'Hey, you!' He was bent double like an inverted U. 'You, boy!' He motioned his head to a ten-year-old boy who was grinning sheepishly with his cheek against a tombstone. 'You! Come here and help me hold it!'

The boy came forward.

'Put your hand on it for me. I have to blow my nose.'

Antonin placed his foot near the hat. The boy put his hand on it. Antonin put a handkerchief to his nose and blew a loud raspberry between his lips. The noise made the children roar.

By now Antonin had forgotten where he was or who he was. He was completely absorbed with another reality. The reality of a living hat that had to be tamed. Spurred on by his audience, he flicked the hat with his toe.

'Hold on to it, boy,' he shouted as he pretended to blow his nose again. The note, like a sour note on a trombone, went on until the children were once again doubled with laughter.

Then suddenly the boy was sitting on his backside and the hat was in the air.

'It moved. It really moved. I saw it,' he shouted.

'You fool, you let it go!'

The hat seemed to be dancing from one hand to another as Antonin juggled it through the crowd. Another group of children had joined him now and they formed a circle.

Eventually Antonin tamed the hat. He placed both hands on it. It jumped up.

He placed one foot on it. 'You stay still or else . . . !' he shouted at it.

'He's got it now,' a boy shouted. 'Hey, mister, want some rope?'

Antonin placed his other foot on the brim. He clapped his hands and grinned.

Then he looked around at each face. All the children's eyes were on the hat. He folded his arms in triumph. With the timing that experience had taught him, he waited. The eyes of the children began to dart up to his own.

'He's going to be quiet now,' said Antonin. 'He's beaten. There's no more mischief left in him.'

But the words were hardly out of his mouth when the hat suddenly sprang into the air and landed with perfect accuracy on Antonin's head, covering his eyes.

The children were jumping up and down and banging their hands on their sides in excitement.

Slowly Antonin's hand went up to the hat. In the last ten

centimetres the hand made a dash for it. Then the other hand came up. Antonin put the hat between his knees and threaded an imaginary needle. He took the thread and pulled it through one side of the hat.

'This'll teach you to stay on!' he said.

Putting the hat on his head, he then threaded the needle through his ear and stitched the hat to one side of his head.

He bit the thread with his teeth and then stitched the other side. He smiled in triumph and strutted around the group pointing to his victory.

There was a warmth about the faces that Antonin had not experienced in a long time. His stomach felt good and his hands were not shaking. Without turning his head too much he looked around the entranced group. The end of the act was simple. And now was the time for it.

He patted the hat and walked towards the cemetery gate. He turned to wave. The children – all watching intently – waved back.

As Antonin turned back, his head purposely struck a low branch on a tree and the hat fell over his eyes. He stamped his foot and cursed loudly. The children roared.

He walked through the cemetery gates to the sound of them running after him laughing.

Just outside the gate was an old man.

'Sir, this is a cemetery! I would ask you to be quiet. Have you no respect for the dead?'

Antonin placed his hat firmly on his head. He looked round again. The children were gathered at the gate. They were forbidden to come outside without an escort.

He walked with his head high, and with the old man shouting further chastisements at him. It was the best morning he had had since he had returned to Prague.

7

It was after four when Antonin reached his apartment. He had paid his agent, Louis, another visit. And he had been to the free market and had managed to get some potatoes.

The potatoes were now boiling. The gas pressure was so low that they would take nearly an hour. Antonin spread a small white tablecloth on the round table in the centre of the room and set a place for himself. From the bureau he took the last gramme of liver sausage. He noticed that Pavel had left some coffee. He decided to make a meal of it and boil that too.

With hungry anticipation he awaited the potatoes. At five minutes to five he turned on the radio softly. As soon as it had warmed up, he set the dial to London. The broadcast in Czech came on at five o'clock.

The booming notes of the beginning of Beethoven's Fifth Symphony filled the room as he sat down to his meal. He turned the radio down.

The news was bad. The Germans were making heavy air raids on London. The local news from Prague which filtered through from the British Intelligence was equally bad. A new German Kommandant had been appointed. Reimann had been replaced. There was news of two Transports which were due to leave the following morning and a warning that stricter curfews were about to be enforced.

At that point in the news there was an unexpected knock on the door.

Antonin sat like a statue. The knock came again. He switched off the radio. With his napkin still tucked into his shirt he opened the door a few centimetres.

A young man in his early thirties was outside. He was dressed in a shiny black raincoat and he carried a soft leather attaché case under his left arm. He took his hat off, revealing heavy Slovak features and light, wavy hair.

'Mr Antonin Karas?'

33

The man put his right hand to the door and pushed it open. Antonin's hands were shaking. He held them against the door.

'My name is Tarchuck, Jiri Tarchuck. I would like to talk to you. About your career. Your career in the theatre.'

The man was inside the door now and Antonin found himself standing aside to let the man close it. He was taller than he had appeared outside. The man's eyes roamed the room quickly.

'I understand you're now free from your work in the theatre?'

'I'm resting.'

'Oh, I see I interrupted your meal. May I sit down? This won't take long.'

'Yes, please sit down. I was nearly finished.'

The man did not sit down immediately. He walked round the room to the chair on the other side of the table. He stopped momentarily in front of the radio.

'Did I disturb your listening?'

Antonin swallowed.

'I was trying to find the right station.'

The man sat down. He spread the raincoat away from his legs and placed his attaché case on his lap. He drew a cigarette from his pocket.

'I'm sure you were. Smoke?'

Antonin took a cigarette. He was trying to hold his hand steady.

'I'm from the office of the Reichsprotektor.' He held out a card. Antonin lit his cigarette and sat at the table. The card trembled in his hand, so he put it firmly on the table.

'There is no need to be frightened. I've come on a friendly visit. I have work to offer you.'

The mask! Pray God for the mask, thought Antonin.

'I'm not frightened. I'm busy. I have contracts coming up here in Prague.' –

'That may be so, but as far as I can see you are free. I've checked with your agent.'

'These things take time, Mr ... ?'

'Tarchuck. Jiri Tarchuck.'

'Tarchuck. Sorry. While it's true that I've nothing booked for a few weeks. ...'

'We heard about your last performance at Klatovy.'

'What performance?'

'You know the one I mean.'

34

Antonin blinked. Could it be that the news had travelled this far?

'The salute!'

The man flicked his cigarette into the ashtray which he now held in his lap.

Antonin took a sip of coffee. He could feel his own skin prickling under his shirt. Christ! If he ever needed the mask, he needed it now!

The man sat forward suddenly and smiled.

'It's all right. I haven't come to arrest you. I'm not interested in such foolish things. We need you.'

'Need me?' Why in hell couldn't he think of something to say?

'To do some entertaining.'

'Entertain? Where? How?'

The man put the ashtray on the table and placed his cigarette in it. The smoke curled up towards Antonin's face. His eyes followed the man's actions as he opened his briefcase and took out a small bottle of cognac.

'I brought this all the way from France. You will join me?'

He took Antonin's glass and poured some into it.

'You have another glass?' He pointed to the sideboard. Automatically Antonin rose and handed him the glass.

'Now let me tell you. *Na zdravi!*' He raised his glass to his lips.

'*Na zdravi!*'

'We wish you to entertain at a children's centre.'

'I am not an entertainer for children,' Antonin snapped back. The mask was coming into place.

'But why shouldn't you entertain children? Your colleagues will envy you.'

'I have no wish to do it, that's why.'

'It's a pity, because within a month all the agencies and theatres are to be closed and you will be working in an arms factory or digging trenches.'

'I still don't understand you.'

'Take another drink. It is good, is it not?'

Antonin finished his cognac.

'As you may have heard on the news from London we have a new Reichsprotektor. There is an edict going out. The theatres are to be closed in retaliation.'

'For what?'

'Certain foolish activities among the people. Bombings and resistance.'

'But who do I entertain then? If the theatres are to be closed?'

'We want you to go to Terezin.'

The word struck Antonin with a sudden sickness from which he found it difficult to recover. He coughed and hid his shaking with his hand to his mouth.

'Too long on that damp farm circuit! Have some more cognac. Yes, at Terezin. As you know the camp was set up there for the Jewish people specifically under the directions of the Führer. It is self-governing and a model state. It is also an important example of the Führer's charity towards the Jewish people. You will see.'

'I refuse. I absolutely refuse.'

Antonin heard his own voice coming back at him. It was like talking in an empty theatre.

'I could tell you a lot more about Terezin, but you and I have heard it all. Have we not?'

The man's continual smile was beginning to make Antonin very angry.

'I'm afraid you have come to the wrong man, Mr . . . '

'Tarchuck. Jiri Tarchuck. You will be able to work at your own profession. We are offering you this opportunity. We know what a great artist you are and there is to be a visit soon at Terezin from the International Red Cross. So you will have an audience of international calibre.'

Antonin stood up.

'Please, I must ask you to leave.'

'I'm afraid I cannot leave.' The man stood up also. 'Please sit down again. Your mother was Jewish, was she not?'

'Yes.'

'Then it is already decided.'

'I will not do this.'

'You will. The car is waiting outside.'

The man pulled aside the curtain.

'There you see. You will either go voluntarily, in which case when you have finished your engagement you will be free, or you will go forcibly and that would mean your staying there.'

The man lit another cigarette.

'You had better collect your things. I shall be downstairs. You will be doing a great service to your own Jewish people.'

He moved to the door and opened it.

36

'You will be making them laugh. And after all why shouldn't they laugh?'

He squashed the cigarette into the linoleum with his shoe.

Ten minutes later a guard and a driver came up to collect Antonin's suitcase. his violin and his make-up kit.

Three old people stood on the street and watched Antonin get into the car. They were still standing motionless as it sped away into the dusk.

Sunset found Antonin travelling in the back seat of the car beside Tarchuck. They were going west. The car had gone north through Prague, turned west over the ring of hills that surround the city, and was now on the plain; a long straight, flat road, lined with apple trees. The naked branches of the trees were like a child's scribbling against the setting sun.

The driver of the Tatra was an SS man. He was humming a waltz. Bristles of hair stood out on his red neck.

Tarchuck smoked constantly and the heat from the rear-mounted Tatra engine gave the car a sickly warmth.

Antonin was angry. He knew it was of little use to argue with Tarchuck. The man had not revealed more than a tight-lipped smile since they had left the apartment.

Occasionally Tarchuck spoke in German to the SS driver. He never addressed Antonin.

At one point Antonin put his hand into his pocket for a cigarette, but sensed it was better to save them. He had managed to secrete three packages in his violin case.

Forty kilometres out of the city the car slowed down to walking pace behind a convoy of German tanks and other military vehicles. Momentarily Antonin thought he might leap from the car into the ditch. But the handles had been taken off the insides of the doors and they could only be opened from the outside.

The SS man spoke: *'Ich habe es erfasst! Die Reise beginnt!'* He grinned into the rear view mirror at Tarchuck and swerved on to the other side of the road. He floored the accelerator. The car went from fifteen kilometres to eighty in a few seconds. The convoy of tanks thundered along in the same direction like a slow train beside them. It twisted round the bends ahead. Antonin's knuckles whitened on the seat.

Around the first bend he could see that the convoy stretched far ahead. The driver must be mad.

'*Was machen Sie?*' he asked.

The driver laughed.

Antonin shut his eyes. The driver and Tarchuck were both laughing, but Antonin could tell they hadn't expected the convoy to be this long. There was no turning into it if something came on the other side of the road.

The tank tracks had turned the road's surface into furrows. The lorries, filled with grim-faced Germans, bounced along beside them.

At last, Antonin, who had shut his eyes, felt the car lurch again to the right and the driver shouted '*Alles gute!*'

Tarchuck was doubled up with laughter now. The danger was over, and he had been scared.

Antonin looked up. The red fortress walls of Terezin's smaller camp were in view.

During the last minutes of the drive Antonin's thoughts had been racing back to the history books of his school days. There were two fortresses at Terezin. Both had been built by the Empress Maria Theresa in the days of the Austrian Empire. They stood on either side of the river, the smaller on the eastern bank and the larger, designed to take up to five thousand men, slightly farther north on the other side.

The walls were so thick that there were houses and barrack rooms inside them, and soldiers could march twenty abreast along their tops. The walls stood about twelve metres high and the two fortresses were joined by a tunnel under the river.

If Antonin's memory served him correctly, they had never been used in a war. Ironically they now housed what was rumoured to be over sixty thousand people.

Each fortress had one gate, a great hole in the massive walls, big enough for the largest lorry to pass through.

It was the gate to the large fortress at which the car had now stopped. With characteristic accuracy the Germans had put a sign up: *Der Eingang.*

Tarchuck handed the SS driver a brown manilla envelope. The driver stepped out of the car, saluted the lieutenant in charge of the gate sentries and handed over the envelope.

The lieutenant had a clip board. He tore open the envelope, read the order inside and ticked something off on a check list on the clip board.

'The office of the Lagerkommandant is to your right, under the arch and keep . . .'

'I am well aware of that, Herr Leutnant,' snapped the SS driver. He climbed smartly back into the car and the gate rolled back on its hinges.

Antonin found himself facing what appeared to be a small town.

Row upon row of parallel streets, grey in the twilight, and

running with checkerboard accuracy, stretched out ahead. The gate slammed behind.

The driver switched on his headlights. To the left, shielding the town itself from the roadway and the wall, was a tall barbed-wire fence with a sentry box high up on the corner. Antonin could just make out the movement of a few people on the other side. Otherwise the place seemed deserted.

The car did not move smoothly. It seemed to glide about as if on ice. Antonin looked through the back window. They were travelling along a sunken railway line in the middle of the road. It stretched back to the gateway like a tram track. The line had been recently built and he wondered why he had not noticed it on the other side of the entrance.

It had been a long time since Antonin had tried to analyse his feelings. It was as if he had been tied to a rope ladder for the last year, spending his total energy trying to climb it. At the top of the rope was the security which had once been his in the theatre. Nothing else had mattered since his wife died. Few other things had even been noticed. His complete preoccupation had obliterated even the war, which had become no more than another obstacle on the rope. And he knew, in his quieter moments, that his efforts had lost him many things, including his friends. His efforts had become an obsession. If he could succeed everything would fall back into place again and his life would be balanced and enjoyable. So far all this had had only one effect. It had made him tired. So tired that he wanted to die. It was only the mask that had saved him.

The car had turned to the right along the south side of a small square. It came to an abrupt stop.

Perhaps it was the slamming finality of the gate closing behind them, or the attitude of Tarchuck in his apartment, or perhaps even the sight of the back of the SS driver's neck, but something clicked abruptly inside Antonin. It was a good, clean feeling. A real emotional response. One which he alone wanted and he alone had conjured up. One which he was going to use. It was like feeling your body hit a cold lake. It was anger. Cold anger.

Tarchuck was shaking his arm. 'Come on, get out!'

Antonin turned to him and their eyes met. The anger in them hit Tarchuck so hard that Tarchuk's eyes went immediately to his briefcase.

41

'The Lagerkommandant is waiting,' he said quietly.

Antonin let his eyes bore into Tarchuck's skull. Tarchuck looked up again once, as Antonin climbed over him and out of the door held by the waiting SS man. Tarchuck was a whipped dog. And every ounce of Antonin was filled with anger.

10

The building which housed SS headquarters at Terezin had once been an officers' mess. Its exterior was still garnished with the trappings of the gay days of a couple of centuries ago.

The hallway inside was wide and handsome. To the right was a double door with ormolu handles, and gilt decorations. Two sentries stood on either side and a woman secretary in SS uniform sat at a small table just in front.

Tarchuck handed her another brown envelope. She slit it open skilfully with a small stiletto. She looked at Antonin with impersonal eyes and rose with the open envelope. The door opened and shut behind her almost silently.

Antonin looked at Tarchuck. Tarchuck was sweating. His fingers had made wet marks on his patent leather briefcase. He coughed and wiped his lips with the back of his hand.

The girl came back. No smile. She held the door open with her left hand. Antonin noticed the wedding ring. It was heavy quality gold and very wide. It seemed slightly large for her finger.

Tarchuck started. In anger, Antonin cut in front of him in the doorway.

The Lagerkommandant was seated at his desk. There was nothing ostentatious about him. His desk was simple. His papers neat and his uniform surprisingly undecorated.

He looked at Antonin who clutched his violin and suitcase. 'So, you've come to entertain the children?'

'I demand my immediate return to Prague,' Antonin said loudly.

The Lagerkommandant did not answer.

Antonin said it again, louder this time. Antonin waited. Then the man smiled softly. He noticed the high cheek bones and deep set blue eyes. His hair was worn quite long for a German and his hands were strong and well manicured.

There was a smell of antiseptic in the room.

The Lagerkommandant suddenly stood up. 'Hat!'

Antonin blinked.

'I said . . . hat!'

Tarchuck put his sweating hand on Antonin's head. 'It is necessary to remove your hat before any person in uniform,' he said, putting the hat on top of Antonin's violin case.

'You will please return me to the car or I shall complain to the authorities,' said Antonin.

The Lagerkommandant took out a cigarette.

'My name is Lagerkommandant Bürger. What equipment have you brought with you?'

'I refuse to answer.'

'Just his violin and some make-up, sir,' said Tarchuck.

The smoke from the cigarette was curling up in front of the Lagerkommandant's eyes.

He sat down again.

'And the rest of your possessions?'

Antonin did not answer. He was determined to let his anger burn itself out.

'His possessions are in his flat in Prague, sir.'

'You have the address, Tarchuck?'

'Naturally, sir.'

'You will see that they come to no harm. Now, Herr Karas . . . to business. Please be seated.' He looked at Antonin again and Antonin noticed something that changed his attitude. 'He's Ales!' he thought, 'the same attitude – and my attitude is beginning to be the same as with Ales. Only this man's a German.'

He lowered himself into a chair.

'There is no need for us to behave in an uncivilised manner. First, you will be paid a fee. No doubt your own government, represented here by Herr Tarchuck, has already discussed the matter with you. . . . '

'I do not want a fee and I refuse to entertain.'

Antonin put his foot against the edge of the desk in his emphasis. A growl came from under it. He looked down. A large, well-fed Alsatian lay there. He noticed that Bürger's boot was gently rubbing the animal's stomach as he talked.

'This is a Jewish State. We have our own bank at Terezin and our own money. Jewish crowns for Jewish people.'

Antonin suddenly wanted a cigarette. The mask was beginning to slip now that his anger had begun to dissipate. He should have held it in, not shouted. He took one from his pocket and searched for a match.

Bürger was watching him intently. He let Antonin take the first puff. Then he said, 'Here, smoking is punishable by death.'

Tarchuck stepped forward to take the cigarette away.

The Lagerkommandant raised his hand to signal him to stop.

'After all, Herr Karas is a visitor. He will be with us only a short time.'

Bürger got up and went over to the window. It was barred, and outside was only the blue sky of night. The Alsatian followed, his claws clicking on the linoleum flooring. He lay again behind his master.

Antonin began, 'I really must insist. . . . '

'You will not insist. You have no right to insist. And it has already been decided. You will entertain the children for the visit by the Red Cross. There will be no arguing! And afterwards you will be returned to Prague.'

Antonin was shaking now. Where had the anger gone? Where was the mask?

'How long will I be here? I have engagements I've promised to fulfil.' He was shouting, but in panic this time.

'Your attitude is unfortunate and I would ask you to behave as a gentleman and not to shout. Your papers please?'

Antonin hesitated. After all the man had a right under orders of the Reichsprotektor to see them.

The Lagerkommandant came to his side. 'The papers?'

Antonin produced them. He took them and put them in the top drawer of his desk. Then he sat down again.

'They will, of course, be returned to you when you leave.'

'But I have a right to have them with me.'

'I've already told you. You have no rights. However, I give you my personal word of honour as a German officer that you will not be kept here at Terezin and that the papers will be returned to you when you leave.'

He pressed a bell on his desk and his secretary came in.

'See that Herr Karas is conducted to his quarters, and that Fraülein Lydrakova is introduced to him so that they can make the final arrangements for entertaining the children.'

He paused and looked at Antonin's violin, 'You can play classics on that?'

'I spent four years at the Prague Conservatory of Music.'

'I shall be delighted to hear you play sometime. We have an excellent orchestra here. One of our cooks used to direct the Prague symphony. Now, Herr Tarchuck, you will convey my regards to all at headquarters. Good day.'

Antonin watched Tarchuck bow his way out. He now felt overwhelmed. He was in the middle of a bad dream.

The Lagerkommandant's secretary said: 'Herr Kommandant, Stürmführer Surgeon Teufel is ready.'

'It's an amputation, isn't it?'

'Yes, sir.' She nervously adjusted her loose wedding ring.

'Then tell him I'll be right along.' He started to draw on some gloves. The dog followed him round the desk. The two sentries saluted at the door and Antonin could hear him say, 'Nothing must go wrong with this special visit. We have orders directly from Berlin.'

Antonin found himself staring after the man. He stood up and placed his hat on his head. How many days ago was it in the cemetery with the children? A week? A year? He shuffled forward and the sentries followed behind. The secretary in her stubby heels led the way, out through another door, and then to a room facing on to the street at the back of the SS headquarters.

'Your food will arrive in a few minutes,' she said and closed the door. He stood listening to her stocky feet echoing in the empty corridor outside the door.

A single electric bulb hung from the ceiling. He put his things on the wooden bed. He turned to the door. It was unlocked. Peering out, he saw two sentries at the end of the windowless corridor. He closed the door. Who – if anyone – were in the other rooms, he wondered?

11

Antonin, shut alone in his room, ceased to think. Impressions were still sweeping in on him. The white-washed walls, the straw mattress, the enamelled bucket in the corner by the small high window, the home-made table in the centre of the room, and beside it the crude three-legged stool. These he saw. Nothing much registered.

Outside in the street, a few shuffling footsteps through the darkness. Somewhere above in the SS headquarters, the sounds of an accordion. There was no point of focus.

A fly settled on the cord of the electric light. It sat rubbing its two front feet together and patting the sides of its face, cleaning it. After a while, the fly went through the light beam and he lost it. Then he began to wonder if there really was a fly or if it had been his imagination playing tricks. Perhaps it was an extension of his act? He stood up and tried to look for it. He thought he saw it in the corner by the urinal pail, but when he went close it was a black mark on the white-wash.

He jerked around hoping to catch sight of it. He stepped back and hit his leg on the table. He saw it – or at least he thought he did – on the top of the straw mattress, but once again it wasn't there. He could hear it though. Surely that was it? Like the drone of an aircraft, always behind him?

'God damn you! Where are you?' he said aloud.

His eyes were no longer on the wall searching for the fly, but on the face of an old man standing inside his door and holding a tin tray with some tin plates and a mug on it. It was a strange face, small and already carved for death. A claw-like hand thrust the tray at him.

Antonin, still dazed, took it and put it on the table. When he turned back again the old man was still standing there.

'Who are you?' he asked.

The old man stood at attention. His eyes were on the bed. The violin was attracting him.

47

'I am 34592, sir,' he said.

'You don't have to stand to attention.'

'Yes, sir.' But he didn't move. His toothless gums rubbed together as he glanced from the violin to Antonin.

'How long have you been here?'

'A long time, sir . . . yes, it's a long time.'

'Do you live here in this building?'

'No, sir. I live in Q 124.'

'What's that?'

'All the streets running . . . you might say . . . east and west . . . they're called by letters. I live on "Q" in house 124. But they're renaming the street.'

His eyes were on the violin once more.

'Why are they renaming the street?'

The old man didn't seem to hear. Antonin repeated the question.

'It's this Red Cross visit, sir. All the streets are being given names . . . there's Lakeview, and Pleasant Avenue and Seabreeze Road.'

'But there's not a lake within fifty kilometres!'

'Sounds better though, doesn't it, sir? I mean with all the officials coming and all that!'

There was a pause.

'Sir, do you play the violin?'

'Yes.' Antonin opened up the case, the old man's coarse breath on his neck.

'You want to watch it, sir . . . that violin . . . they'll steal anything round here . . . your watch too, I shouldn't wonder.'

Antonin went back to the table. There was a slice of black bread and some soup in the plate. The tin cup had tea in it. 'Look. You take the food. I don't want it.'

'It's not allowed.'

'Then take it away. I'm not hungry.'

'No, sir.'

'Jesus-Maria, take it!'

The old man moved from where he had been standing by the bed and took the tray off the table.

'You just watch out for that violin . . . they're all thieves in this place. There's ninety-two people in 124 and I wouldn't trust one of 'em with my own mother.'

The door closed and Antonin heard him shuffling down the corridor. Then he heard the guards shouting. He flung open the door and the old man was climbing unsteadily to his feet. A sentry had his foot on the tray. The old man was mumbling something. The other sentry lifted his boot and pushed him back on to the tray. The sentry lifted his boot again.

Antonin started to come down the corridor. Two paces down, he stopped. The sweat was out on his brow and he knew that whatever happened he could go no further. He was afraid. He ran back into his room and shut the door. He stood there shaking, hearing the old man cursing and the guards banging their boots. He tried desperately to tell himself that they were only having fun with the old man. And that everything was all right.

Then there was a long silence. He noticed that he had cut his right hand in four places. With his own nails.

He tried to stop the bleeding with his handkerchief. What could he do? No. No. What *should* he do?

What *should* he do? His eyes darted the walls in search of an answer? Do? Act? Something!

He opened the door and looked down the corridor. The old man was no longer there. The sentries stood at ease. The spilled soup was on the floor, but they had obviously made him try to clean it up.

Antonin started to run. As he ran, he gained confidence. He was shouting. Not words. Syllable and animal noises.

The sentries turned.

'Let me go. I'm leaving. Let me go.' His lungs were trained to carry and they did. People came running from other parts of the building. Then something hit him on the neck and everything went black.

He woke to find himself on his straw mattress. The door was closed and he could tell by the way it fitted snugly into its frame that it was now bolted on the other side.

He sat up. . . . His right shoulder was very painful but he could move his arm. He wondered what time it was. His watch seemed to have stopped.

A cigarette! To hell with their rules. He opened his violin case. He had hidden three packs there. All three were gone. He remembered the old man. He'd left him standing by the bed. The old bastard. Finally he remembered what had happened to the old man and he got up and felt ashamed.

Then he saw the fly. It was on the wall about two feet above the urinal pail. He held his breath. Balancing on one leg he took off his left shoe. He moved slowly and softly across.

He caught the fly with the first blow, leaving red, brown and black pulp on the wall. But he hit it until the shoe began to hurt his hand and he had to stop.

His shoulder was painful and he was tired.

He dragged himself on to his mattress and buried his head, weeping until the stench of the sweat of the previous owner forced him to lie and weep on his back.

12

It was barely sunrise at Terezin when the thin form of a fifteen-year-old boy slipped quietly into the boys' dormitory at L 365, now renamed Woodland Road, and started the whispered rumour.

The beds were tiered wooden bunks, like shelves. There were five to a tier which meant that each boy had half a metre of headroom. It had been worked out that as the attic room was fifteen metres long and ten wide, the metre width of each bed, plus the metre foot gap between each row of tiers would allow for the accommodation of one hundred and twenty boys.

'A clown. There's a real clown here in camp. A clown!'

The rumour took less than thirty seconds to pass quietly from head to head round the half-sleeping unventilated room.

It was exciting news. Good news. Today it was known that a Transport would be leaving for the east. The train had been heard shunting the wagons together outside the walls during the night. The names of the people to be put on it would be announced by the Elders of the Jewish State early that morning. They would be rounded up and sent to the Schlojska, a large and much feared hut situated by the railhead inside the camp. And by evening they would all have left. Many of the boys in L 365 still had parents. The news of the clown's arrival did much to take their minds off the day's major event.

The boys and girls under sixteen had been separated from their parents at Terezin some two years previously. The reason, of course, was that their parents could then pursue their own activities unrestricted by the ties of family. The children could be given a modern, hygienic upbringing.

They could also be confined to learning the German language undisturbed.

The girls' dormitories were dotted about the camp. The only difference being that they were permitted from the age of fourteen to perform duties for the soldiers and hence gain special privileges.

Most adults were separated in similar ways, married couples being allowed one visiting night a week, which privilege was removed should the wife become pregnant.

Nevertheless children were born, and some lived long enough to join their parents on the Transports.

At L 365 the news of the clown was coupled with another piece of good gossip. Apparently the girls from M 32 were going to join with them and to put together an entertainment. It was to be bigger and better than the secretly performed pantomime 'Brundebar' which had been such a success the previous year. The entertainment was to be performed in a specially selected part of the camp, boarded off from the rest. International dignitaries, perhaps Herr Goebbels himself, were to be present. And there would be treats. An extra ration of potatoes, even meat and some chocolate.

The Lagerkommandant was to distribute the extra food himself, aided by some of the 'trusties'.

So by and large the good news of the day offset the bad. If you were lucky.

13

To Vera Lydrakova, walking along 'M' street (the new name for which had not yet been announced) towards her girls in M 32, the day had not dawned so well. To begin with, it was damp and the clouds had thickened over the tops of the barely visible hills to the north just over the walls of the camp. This meant rain or, worse, snow.

She had been always very much affected by the weather ever since she had been a small girl living on Strahovska street, near the castle in Prague. It always set her mood for the day. Today there was the news that they were hunting out people for another Transport to the East. It would be mostly the old or political prisoners who would go. Vera hadn't a relative to lose. They had all already died or been taken away. She had only herself to protect, and she was young, tall and still filled with energy. She played upon Bürger's unconcealed liking of her to help work small miracles for her girls. But she knew the day would come when Bürger would demand his reward from her. Meanwhile Bürger made no attempt that could not be resisted, busying himself with others and under the watchful eye of his own beautiful young daughter.

So Vera occupied herself as hopefully as she could.

As she walked she noticed that already the older people were out in line with their tins for the potato soup which the cooks were dishing out at the end of 'M'. They would stand in line for an hour or more, while the soup lasted. It was served from an old oil drum on a home-made cart.

Vera smiled and waved at them. She felt a little better now. The depression definitely had been the weather. She must pull herself together. The Transport had yet to be faced. All morning they would be collecting up the people and handing out the cards with the numbers on them to hang around their necks.

It would take all the strength she had to keep the minds of the children away from the sounds of all this in the street. Some of them would undoubtedly lose somebody. It was a matter of living through the day.

'I have become a stone,' she said to herself. The alternative would have been to become blind and deaf. And being a stone is better.

There were some sparrows pecking away at the crumbs of bread which fell on the cobblestone road as the cooks broke bread for the old people's soup.

14

Antonin sat on the edge of his bed. It had been a long, cold night. The dampness made his clothes stick to his body. His mind jogged along from subject to subject. Old jokes, worn-out routines, the smell of the green room at a country theatre, his mother baking bread, running to school with the snow crunching like taut rubber under his boots . . . his apartment with the knick-knacks he loved on the mantelshelf . . . the picture of his wife.

But it was no good! He was here. At Terezin. He struggled to bring his brain into focus. To face the fact. But it kept slipping back into the muddy waters of his memories. The cracks and corners. Anywhere but here. It was like knowing you had to rehearse. You did everything in your power to try to start, but you also kept putting it off. Changing your clothes, going to the washroom, having a drink, picking up ashtrays and emptying them, sweeping the rug.

His eye caught sight of his shoe beside the pail.

If they made him do his act. If they forced him to work for them. He would just stand in silence. They would probably shoot him. But that didn't matter very much. Yes, it did. It mattered a lot. He didn't want to be shot.

He picked up the shoe and wriggled it on over his damp sock. And another thing . . . that man Bürger, the Lagerkommandant, he had promised. And Antonin had no reason to believe that he didn't mean it. A short stay to entertain while the Red Cross came to the camp. And then back to Prague. It was work, wasn't it? And probably well paid too, although he didn't understand about this money business. A bank here in the camp?

The lace in his shoe broke. Laces were hard to get. He tied the broken ends together and laced up the shoe. And anyway . . . the people here . . . did someone say there were 60,000? . . . probably could do with a laugh. Of course he'd talk to Bürger and explain that he was not a children's entertainer. It would have to be two shows a night for adults. Bürger was a man of his word. He'd respect his wish. Obviously. Hadn't he asked him to play the violin for him . . . and classics too?

'Get up and follow me. *Ich habe es eilig.*'

An SS man was standing beside him.

'My breakfast?'

'*Später!*' The man was smoking a cigarette. The smell brought a craving into Antonin's mouth. 'First you will come with me,' the soldier said.

Antonin picked up his violin and his hat. The make-up box? He picked that up too.

The SS man led Antonin out on to the street from the back entrance of the Gestapo headquarters.

It was the first time he'd seen Terezin in daylight. The street was exceptionally grey, and it ran the length of the fortress, from wall to wall. It was about two-thirds of a kilometre long, and straight as a die. The buildings on either side were cold walls in themselves, shuttered and intersected with mathematical exactitude by other similar streets. Before the war these grim buildings had housed the military garrison and those who had provisioned it, merchants, market people, haberdashers and clothiers.

The SS man caught Antonin's arm and pushed him forward along the street towards the western wall.

There was little sign of life. Yet it was not early. A few old people still waited by the soup drums. Antonin briefly caught sight of a very small child at a window.

The SS man's highly-polished boots echoed on the cobbles = to the sounds of an empty town of sixty thousand people? Where were they all?

Finally, after two blocks, Antonin came across two men changing the name place of the street. They had painted out the old one and had already put in PIN. . . . Antonin supposed it was something like Pine Street. He shouted good morning to the men but they merely took off their hats as the SS man passed and went on with their work. Their faces were grey, like the walls. Yet they were not old.

At the end of the block Antonin found himself facing a high, wooden fence. The SS man unlocked a small gate set in it. Antonin went through. The gate was locked again on the other side. Ahead was the 'town' square. A carpet of grass stretched towards a big Baroque church. On the left was a town hall. To the right a bank and several shops. In the middle of the grass carpet a bandstand had been put up as well as an open-air theatre. The buildings had been painted recently, and from some of the windows brilliant splashes of chrysanthemums burst like spring air into the cloudy December cold.

The fence behind Antonin, which had been rough plank on the other side, was painted bright green. The small gate they had come through was camouflaged with a mural of spring flowers.

Antonin began to laugh. The Germans had built a film set. They had actually set about to transform the camp into a Jewish paradise. The long green wall was the back-drop. The grass had probably been cut in strips from fields in southern Slovakia and laid on the bare earth. The bright painting on the buildings was tinsel. So this was what the International Red Cross officials and Dr Goebbels were to see? Antonin was still laughing. It was so typical. So exact. So pretty. Even the biggest fool in the whole Red Cross organisation could see it was a fake.

'*Warum lachen Sie?*' The SS man was angry and mystified.

'I'm laughing because . . . this . . . this . . . . ' Antonin could not contain himself. . . . 'It's Hansel and Gretel. A fairy tale!'

When Antonin finally dried his eyes he heard the faint whistle of a train at the other end of the camp.

15

Vera Lydrakova lifted her head. She too heard the train whistle. But she was no longer thinking. She was numb to such intrusions on her daily routine.

The long attic beams that ceilinged her classroom, the home of seventy-nine girls in M 32, were damp with rain. The window, half a metre by two, which had once been a skylight, was covered with blackout cloth so that no German or 'trusty' passing in the street could tell she was teaching. Today the blackout also helped solve another problem. It deadened the street noise which had already begun.

A girl of thirteen, Anna, sat on a little shelf beside the trap door in the floor which led to the stairs and to other parts of the house. She could hear immediately anyone entering the floor below.

Precious possessions cluttered the floor. A cracked earthenware pot with a geranium in it. Some smooth round pebbles. Tattered blankets. A pair of shoes. Linen bags, sewn from hospital sheets, containing matches, pencils, crayons, even small pieces of smooth wood.

Everyone had to have something of her own. Nothing was useless. It mattered only that it was a possession.

The train whistled again. This time it was from within the walls. Vera looked at the faces. There was little visible reaction. But in fact each girl was almost totally occupied with her own worries. The names had not yet been drawn for the Transport. The Elders had sat through the night deciding. There had been secret meetings and deputations. Offers of bribes. Money had undoubtedly changed hands and names had been deleted. Mothers had offered services to save children, or themselves. It was an horrific job for the Jewish Elders. They were supposed to be governors of the camp, and when a Transport left for labour camps in the east the people on it were never heard of again. Not all the Elders were good men. Some were out to save their own skins or to make something from it. It was human nature. Saving yourself had become a way of life in the camp. When one of Vera's children was taken away she would give her possessions to a friend. Were she taken suddenly, as might happen today, the possessions would be stolen almost before she'd left the room.

You could hear the train shunting the cattle wagons into the siding which ran down the middle of 'A' street, next to the Schlojska.

Vera stood up. She had been sitting cross-legged like the rest of the class on the rough attic boards. She must start something going. She must keep minds busy.

Vera's legs were too long for the attic, and she had to stoop. Ever since a child she had been acutely conscious of her body. Its firm flesh pleased her, but today it prickled with nervousness.

Seventy-nine Stars of David faced her. She shook free her fair hair, a habit from the days when it had been allowed to grow down her back. Now it was shorter than most boys'.

The trick was to keep the girls' minds on tomorrow. To pretend that there would always be a tomorrow. A tomorrow many years ahead.

Within a few minutes she had an ardent discussion going. The children lapped up anything. Learning was an entertainment.

She heard herself saying, 'It may *sound* fantastic but such a thing is possible. Last night I was speaking to Dr Koch. . . . '

Maria, a well-developed girl of eleven, interrupted her.

'You mean land on the moon?' Her eyes were large with wonder. Only Jana, at the back of the attic, was not looking at her. Jana was writing seriously.

'Not only to land on it, but to have people living on it. Anna, what is the most important element to overcome in such an expedition?'

Anna wrinkled her brow. Then shrugged. The children giggled. Anna liked to play soccer with the boys. Her mind was rarely in class.

'Maria, what do you think?'

'Dunno.'

'Does anyone know?'

All sorts of hands went up.

'Luba?'

'Miss Lydrakova, it might be air?'

'Right, oxygen. We will have to wear some sort of suit that would have a supply of oxygen in it.'

'But getting off the ground . . . it's such a long way!' said Luba.

'The earth's gravity will have to be overcome. Can anyone tell me its strength? How strong is the earth's pull?'

They were shouting in the street now and Vera could hear the sound of steel-tipped boots on the cobbles. The list had been announced.

'Quickly, someone . . . Luba?'

'The earth's gravity pulls at 980 centimetres a second.'

'Correct. And how high above the earth's surface does it go?'

Maria's dark eyes met Vera's. Maria too was thinking of something to keep her mind occupied. Vera could see the emptiness in her eyes. 'Right to the moon?' said Maria.

'No.'

A few hands were shaking at her trying to get her attention. She wondered what it was that Jana was writing so busily? She hadn't stopped since the class began.

Outside in the street, doors were banging and orders were being shouted in German. Everything had to be carried out at a run.

'No, Maria, it's about a hundred kilometres only. After that there's no air.'

'But if you missed the moon, you'd go on and on forever.'

'The men who go will have to be very brave. But after a while things will be worked out mathematically so that anyone will be able to travel there. Once you are in space – according to Dr Koch – and pointed the right way, it would be hard to miss the moon.'

There was laughter now.

Vera walked to the window and lifted the blackout curtain. 'How many of you really believe that one day we'll reach the moon?' She dared not look back a them. There was a tense silence in the room. Outside in the street thirty people were being herded into lines, counted and recounted.

Vera turned to the class again. They all knew what was happening outside, yet they wanted to play the game with her.

'You didn't hear me. I asked how many believe we'll get there?'

Six hands went up.

'Only six of you?'

'I know it's impossible,' said Luba.

'Nothing is impossible.'

'Well it is. That's why,' said Luba. 'God didn't mean it.'

'I think God meant it, Luba. He meant us to explore the whole universe. What sort of a world would you like to build out there in space?'

Luba said, 'One where everyone has a room of her own.'

'And lots of chocolate cake,' said Anna. 'The biggest chocolate cake in the world.'

The class laughed again. People laughed at almost anything these days.

Maria said, 'Yes . . . and where there'll be no fighting.'

'And no boys,' added Freda from the back of the class.

There was laughter again.

Jana lifted her eyes. They met Vera's. But there was no message in them. She immediately went back to her writing.

Vera said, 'Well, I wouldn't like it without boys.'

'We wouldn't last very long alone!' said Maria seriously.

'That's right. There'd be no babies,' said Luba. The class consensus was that boys should stay.

Vera heard another round of shouting in the street. She couldn't hold herself back. She lifted the curtains again. The end of the block seemed to be the meeting place for the march to the Schlojska.

'How many are they taking?' asked Anna suddenly.

'Just a few.'

'When's the Transport leaving?' asked Luba. There was no emotion in her voice.

'Oh, sometime tonight, I guess,' said Maria.

Vera sensed the tension growing. If only they hadn't come back for more. The classroom had been missed the first time. But there was always the chance that there would be substitutions. Up until the time the train left you were never sure.

Vera said, 'Maybe after the war, if we land on the moon it will bring all nations closer together and there'll be no more war and people will live happily.'

'Well, if they don't want fighting they'd better let women govern,' said Anna.

This brought a roar of laughter from the class and Vera had to hold up her hand for silence.

'Well, I don't see why women can't govern,' said Maria.

'In my home, when I get married, I'm going to govern. My husband is going to obey me,' said Luba.

61

Vera couldn't keep her hands still and the false bantering of the children was getting her down. She wanted to shout at them to shut up. Or just to run out of the room and leave them. Run. Anywhere.

'There's someone coming!'

Anna said it quite loudly. It was routine. Everyone had to hear. All teaching papers were slipped away and song books in German came out. It was done with care and precision.

As they struck up the first bars of 'O, Tannenbaum,' which happened to be the page Vera opened her book at, the head of an SS man came through the trap door. The class immediately stopped singing and stood up to attention. The air was electric.

'Fräulein Lydrakova? You will please step outside.'

'Very well children, you may be seated,' said Vera, 'and keep on with the singing. Only choose something else Luba. Something more in keeping.'

Vera tried to appear calm. There was bad news ahead. If only her hands would stop shaking. The nervous habit of tossing back her hair started again. She went down the stairs to the landing below.

Antonin was standing there waiting for her.

16

Upstairs in the classroom a soft lullaby was being sung. It was the Terezin song. It had special words to it. It was always sung when there was trouble.

Anna said quietly to Luba, 'Something is happening. What is it?'

'Another Transport. He's probably come to get someone.'

'There'll be shooting,' said Maria.

'There was shooting this morning,' said Freda.

Marta, a pretty girl of thirteen with dark brown eyes and crinkly blonde hair, looked up from her drawing.

'They shot Branich and Husak.'

'Maybe the war's over and we'll all go home.'

'Yeah, or live on the moon!' said Maria.

'You'll all go to the labour camps in the east. All of us will. Now shut up and let's really sing.'

The swelling song, which suddenly burst into Czech instead of German, could be heard by Antonin and Vera below.

17

The SS man, whose official new task was director of public relations for the camp, had introduced Antonin to Vera. He had told Vera to take Antonin to the boys' residence at L 365 as soon as possible and had given orders to start preparing the entertainment immediately. He had also handed Vera a slip of paper which was an official document from Bürger's office. It also had the stamp of the Jewish Elders on it. She was glancing at it now.

She folded it and put it in her dress pocket.

'Well, Mr Karas, let us start . . . '

'You understand it is against my will.'

'Everything here is.'

'After the Red Cross visit I shall return to Prague. I have many engagements to fulfil.'

'I'm sure. Well, how shall we begin?' She gave an embarrassed smile. 'I see they haven't given you a Star of David yet. You'd better get one. To be without it can be dangerous.'

'Yes, of course,' he coughed nervously. He hadn't expected anyone like Vera. He'd been thinking of a typical school teacher.

'I'm afraid, Mr Karas, that I never had much time to go to the theatre. I studied at art school and spent useless hours in galleries. . . . '

'If you had been a theatre fan you'd have heard about me, I expect.' Antonin did not mean to sound proud. He was unduly nervous. He continued, 'I've never entertained children. I told the Lagerkommandant but he's making me do it.'

'The man's a complete fool. So you aren't used to children?'

'It's not that. I'm an adult entertainer. All my material is designed with sophistication. . . . '

'Well, I've been trying to find the secret for years too and I still hope to one day. In the meantime we're in the same boat. Listen to them.'

'They say that there's a Transport. . . . '

'Yes. It leaves tonight. Before we go to the boys, would you like to see my girls? We teach each day and when they interrupt we pretend to draw or sing.'

Vera banged the trap door. Two longs and a short. It opened.

Antonin said, 'Forgive me if I sound strange. Everything is new . . . and well, frankly I didn't expect to find anyone like you here.'

Vera was ahead of him on the stairs. He was noticing her legs.

'You're a bit of a shock too, Mr Karas.' He laughed again nervously.

'I suppose so. I'm glad we're working together = although I still object to it. Very strongly. But if it has to be then I'm glad it's you.'

18

As Vera pulled herself through the trap door, the class rose.

'This is Mr Antonin Karas, the famous comedian. He's a clown and he's come to entertain us. As you know we're all putting on a play with the boys.'

There was a chorus of 'Good morning Mr Karas'.

'You may be seated, girls.' Vera found herself being unusually prim.

Antonin gave a shy little wave. It brought a laugh. Outside they could hear the marching of soldiers' feet again. Steel against stone. Precision.

'You may start drawing,' said Vera. She had positioned herself next to Marta. 'You've already done a drawing, Marta. It's beautiful. Show it to Mr Karas.'

Marta handed Antonin a page from an old exercise book. On it she had drawn a yellow butterfly. It was flying over a wall and the background inside the wall was a dirty brown. Outside there were trees and fields.

'What does it mean?' Antonin asked. It was a stupid question but he could think of no other.

'It's to go with Jana's poem.'

'So that's what you've been doing while we were all off to the moon, Jana,' said Vera, 'can we see it?'

She put her arm round Jana.

'It's nothing.'

'Well, maybe the rest of us would like to see it anyway.'

There was another chorus of 'yeses'.

'All right. But you read it, Miss Lydrakova.'

'Very well,' Vera took the paper. She studied it for a second. Antonin stood embarrassedly beside her.

Vera began:

The last, the very last,
so richly, brightly, dazzlingly
yellow.

Perhaps if the sun's tears
would sting against a
white stone. . . .

Such, such a yellow is carried
lightly 'way up high.

It went away I'm sure because
it wished to kiss the world
goodbye.

For seven weeks I've lived
in here, penned up inside this
ghetto

But I have found my people here.
The dandelions call to me

And the white chestnut candles in the court.
Only I never saw another butterfly.

That butterfly was the last one.
Butterflies don't live in here, in
the ghetto.

There was a pause. Antonin said, 'It's beautiful.'
The class began to clap. Jana flushed and Vera saw the tears
coming to her eyes. She hugged her and Marta came over and
hugged her too.
'You must sign it and show it to Dr Koch. I think he'd like to
keep a copy of it. If he does, he may publish it one day and
you'll be famous.'
'We'll all be famous,' said Anna, 'because we liked it first.'
The class clapped again and started to laugh.
Vera said, 'Well now, I have to take Mr Karas over to see the
boys. . . . '
'Can we come, miss?' someone asked.
'No. I'll be back soon. Keep on drawing and if anyone comes
don't let them in until everything is put away. Luba, you're in
charge.'
As they left the attic the whole class stood up again.

'Goodbye Mr Karas. *Dobry den.*'

'*Dobry den,*' Antonin replied.

Vera and Antonin climbed down the stairs. Vera reached up to close the trap door. Antonin took the door from her. His hand brushed her arm. She blushed.

With the trap door shut they began to go down the corridor to the front stairs, through the small hell holes that housed dozens of adults. Then into the street.

The street was empty. Vera smiled with relief.

'That child is very talented. The poem is truly beautiful.'

'Yes,' said Vera, 'her father was sent to the Transport this morning. That document the SS man gave me. It was his paper. She doesn't know yet.'

'My God. Who will tell her?'

'I will. When I get back. Let's take the short cut through the back of the barracks. They'll be so busy with the damn Transport they'll never see us.'

Antonin followed her quickening step.

19

Here, as he walked along beside the strutting Vera, Antonin saw yet another new life. People at work. He had learned from her already that most of the camp was set to work doing something. The very young cleaned billets. The youths worked in the fields outside the camp, harvesting grain for the soldiers, herding cows and pigs for SS stomachs and keeping sewage ditches cleaned. One woman, Anna Pechkoff, herded the sheep that were now the property of Bürger, but had once been proudly owned by the farmers of Lidice. When the Nazi troops burned Lidice and its inhabitants in reprisal for the death of Heydrich, the hated Protector of all Bohemia, Bürger stole the sheep and had them driven by Anna to Terezin.

Some inmates were lucky enough to work in the hospital. Others worked in the morgue. A despised class of 'trusties' – *kapos*; thugs and criminals turned Nazi foremen – took charge of each work party. They were often more brutal than their SS masters.

But what Antonin saw that morning walking to L 365 were parties of women on their knees on the pavements and roadways along which the visiting dignitaries would travel. They were scrubbing the roads and white-washing walls.

There were very few old people in the streets. Most of them were in hiding or in the Schlojska awaiting departure.

The building L 365 had once been a school for the sons of Czech soldiers. It was a large brown building on the west side of the street. It had become the most powerful and toughest boys' residence in the camp.

Just inside the doorway was a fair haired boy of sixteen, steel eyed and tight lipped.

'Are you the clown?'

'Yes, I am.'

'This is Mr Karas,' said Vera, 'is Mr Capek here?'

69

'He left on the Transport. Come in. We were waiting for you.'

The boy signalled to a comrade down the hall. A whistle, one short and two long shrill calls, sounded up the stairway to the attic.

'Who is in charge of you now,' asked Vera.

'The Elders have not appointed anyone yet.' The boy's eyes were on Antonin's watch. 'I'll give you twenty potatoes for it,' he said.

'I don't wish to sell it,' said Antonin.

'Very well,' the boy shrugged as they climbed the stairs, 'but twenty potatoes are better than nothing!'

The look he gave Antonin reminded him of the old man yesterday. He clutched his violin.

The room below the attic where they all slept had once been a major classroom. It was now stripped bare. German posters were on the walls, and on a blackboard some crude drawings of Nazi officers urinating on themselves. The only other decoration was a sheet of paper announcing names for a soccer match to be held in connection with the visit.

As Antonin and Vera entered the room there was a round of applause.

A boy caught hold of Antonin's arm. 'We want you to meet Jiri.' They were in the middle of one hundred and twenty boys.

The boy pulled harder. 'He's over here.'

'Have you come from Prague?'

'Are the street cars still running?'

'I used to live on Maislova.'

'My dad was in the theatre. He was a lighting man.'

'Hey, can you make us laugh?'

'You don't look funny. Where's your funny face?'

'Didn't they give you a Star?'

'The guy's a bum. Someone they found on the street. Think they'd spend money getting someone to entertain us!'

The questions died as suddenly as they started. A fear crept into the room.

'It's all right. This is Antonin Karas. He is a clown and he's come to help us put on the concert.'

Antonin's eyes roved over the group. Thin faces, twisted faces, faces filled with doubt and uncertainty. Some bullies among them. . . . Some he wouldn't have liked to meet on the street after dark. Others . . . apart from the appalling state of

70

their clothes, were amazingly like children he had recently seen on the streets of Prague.

'Hey, Jiri, do your stuff.'

A small boy. Very dark, his eyes shifting shyly at the floor and one hand scratching his forehead, stood before Vera and Antonin.

Because he could think of nothing better to say, Antonin said, 'What were you doing?'

'Just sort of fooling around.'

'Show him Jiri. Show him your act.'

'Well, do I have to now?'

'You promised.'

'I don't feel like it.'

'You let us down now and you'll get it right up the arse.'

'Get the little bugger and hold him down; that'll make him change his mind!'

'Quiet.' It was Vera. Her voice had an edge on it when she wanted. There was a silence.

Antonin said quietly, 'Come on Jiri, show me what you can do.'

'I was just acting the fool.'

'Then I'll watch.' Antonin sat on the floor.

'No, sir. I'll get into trouble.'

'It's all right,' said Vera. 'You trust me, don't you?'

The boy's eyes sparkled and he suddenly looked into Antonin's face. 'Well . . . all right.'

A chair was passed over the heads of the crowd.

'Give me some room then.'

The crowd pushed back.

Jiri climbed on the chair. He folded his arms. And bowed towards Antonin. The boys around started to titter.

'You just wait. . . . You'll see!'

Jiri then pulled from his pocket a small paint brush, with the handle cut short and the bristles shortened to spikes. He stuck the short handle up his nose. Then he produced a grey wig from his pocket. In a second it was on his head. He was Hitler.

A roar of laughter went up from the crowd and they started to clap. Jiri stomped around the chair and finally fell over the edge; both the wig and the brush went flying.

There was so much laughter in the room that some of the boys were rolling on the floor.

Jiri was beside the chair again now and he was joined by two other boys. One stuffed paper down his jersey and was Goering.

71

The other hobbled along with a pretended club foot as Goebbels.

Jiri suddenly jumped on to the chair. The laughing stopped. This was something new.

Jiri pointed to a boy standing next to Antonin.

'Hang your head, Jew!'

The boy obeyed.

'Come here, Jew!'

The boy shuffled forward, head hanging.

When he arrived in front of the chair Jiri said, 'Jew, you are a dog!'

For a split second Antonin was worried. But the boys burst into round after round of applause and laughter.

Jiri then said, 'On all fours, Jew!'

The boy got down awkwardly.

'Now run around this chair, Jew. Come on, you dog, run!'

The boy began to run round the chair at Hitler's feet. When he had completed three turns and the other boys were no longer laughing, Jiri shouted, 'Come here, Jew! Lick the floor. Lick the floor, I say!'

Once again the boys broke into uncontrollable laughter. Antonin could not understand it. He was smiling politely and trying to look at ease, but the palms of his hands were sweating.

Vera said, 'That's the sort of crudity that stops us all going insane.'

'It's . . . senseless . . . senseless. . . .'

'That's why we need you.'

Antonin was standing now. He looked closely at Vera. Her eyes were pleading with him to understand.

A sudden long whistle from below brought the laughter to an abrupt halt. In seconds the boys were in lines and silently standing while another, bigger boy had taken Jiri's place on the chair.

He was saying, 'I vote we have Murac play centre forward. Anyone against raise his hand.'

None raised a hand.

'Maybe Murac is too sick. How about Jaro?' said someone.

'He went out this morning on the Transport.'

'Hell, we'll have to do with Murac,' said Jiri. Two SS men and a Kapo were standing at the door. No one turned. They knew. Antonin wished he hadn't turned. He felt a traitor.

The men started to go down the stairs again and soon the whistle 'all clear' came again.

72

Antonin bounded up, unwinding himself like a coil of rope. He crooked his index finger at where the SS men had stood. The boys started to laugh again. 'And that too!' he said clenching his fist and driving his arm upwards.

He held up his hand for silence. All eyes were on him. His body sagged. His arms hung limp. Suddenly he jumped to life in his own imitation of Hitler. But it was a Hitler who had got up one morning and lost his moustache, so that he shouted all his orders with a lisp.

Antonin spent a good deal of time on all fours looking for the moustache and when he found it he stuck it on upside-down. Of course there was no moustache, but you could tell it was upside-down because he kept sneezing and trying to get it off again and turn it round. He ended up by suddenly doing a Nazi salute. The crowd slowly became silent. They weren't sure. But Antonin knew what he was doing. Suddenly he said, 'That's how high a Jewish dog can jump – right over a Nazi's arm!'

The boys mobbed him after that and it took him quite a time to reach Vera at the door. Tears of laughter were on her cheeks.

'Now do you understand?' she said.

'I think I do.'

Yesterday he felt anger. Today he felt a certain joy.

'At least I think I do,' he said.

20

While Antonin was doing his act and the train was being prepared for loading, a group of teenage girls had been recruited by a woman SS sergeant to march outside the gates at Terezin and to pick onions for the soldiers' dinner.

One girl, the same Jana who had written the poem, had specially prepared her pants so that she could stuff them with onions when the SS woman, who came with whip and Alsatian dog, wasn't looking. Onions were the most precious commodity at Terezin. They contained nourishment.

For two hours the girls worked filling sacks with onions. Not once were they allowed to stop.

Jana finally said to her friend, 'I've got to do a pee. I'm bursting.'

'Ask the battleaxe. I doubt if she'll let you.'

Jana did. And the battleaxe refused.

Jana said to her friend, 'I can't hold on.' And she urinated standing up. It soaked the onions.

She started to cry.

'Why are you crying?' said her friend.

'I'll have to throw away the onions.'

'Don't you dare, you'll be wasting good food.'

21

At the same time, four people waiting for the Transport to leave, died. They were carted to the morgue near the gate.

The bodies of the two men who were shot that morning were taken from the place of execution in the small fortress and buried in the ditch outside the wall. A small, wrinkled old man rifled their pockets and stripped off their clothing. He also dug the lead bullets out of the stone wall, which the men had been stood up against, and pocketed the lead.

Later that day, the band started rehearsals and the Lager-kommandant opened a candy store on the corner of the square. As yet no one had any money to buy with, as it hadn't been printed for the bank to distribute. That was all due tomorrow. And in any case, the candies had not arrived either. The shipment of Red Cross parcels, usually waylaid in Prague were also due tomorrow. There would be Swiss chocolate inside the parcels.

And still later that day, the onions were enjoyed in an illegal soup by thirty-three people in C 93, now renamed Trout Lake Drive.

Antonin went to bed happy that night. Vera looked forward to tomorrow, and it wasn't until he finally was about to go to sleep that Antonin found that some boy had stolen his watch while he was performing.

Very late that night, the Transport left, slowly puffing its way through the gate; twelve wagons, each with eighty people in it.

22

No one ever disturbed Lagerkommandant Bürger until after he had breakfasted. He lived in a twelve room mansion in the little fortress. It had once belonged to the 17th century General Knäbel. It was rumoured that Maria Theresa had slept there. It stood back from the main parade ground at the fortress, protected in the front by a small white picket fence, a stretch of lawn and some apple trees. Behind the mansion the high walled garden stretched to the eastern end of the wall. Bürger had built a swimming pool here for his daughter.

His wife, who suffered from severe rheumatism had been shipped back to Berlin. The daughter, not nineteen, was mistress of the house, and the apple of her father's eye.

The little fortress was reserved for the more rebellious prisoners. They lived in the holes cut into the high walls and were paraded for recreation once a day passing the mansion in shackles. Day after day Bürger's daughter would stand and watch them.

The little fortress was also the main place of execution. There was a small tunnel, no higher than four feet and not wide enough for a man to turn round in, which went under the wall and just to the north of the mansion. On the other side of the wall, stood the gallows; and a strange pit which prisoners were building with pipes leading to it, not unlike showers.

This particular morning, however, Bürger had not breakfasted when his aide, Leutnant Hoffman, brought him the cable from Berlin.

He stood beside Bürger who was in his braces, sitting having his boots pulled on by an orderly. The cable was in the simplest terms. It read: RED CROSS VISIT POSTPONED UNTIL ARRIVAL OF HERR EICHMANN AT A DATE TO BE ANNOUNCED TO YOU STOP RED CROSS PRESIDENT SUSSENS REFUSES TO VISIT WITHOUT HERR EICHMANN STOP GOEBBELS

Bürger stood up suddenly and kicked away the orderly.

'Christ! After all those preparations!'

'Is there anything I can do, sir?'

'When did you decode this?'

'Ten minutes ago, sir.'

'Is there another copy?'

'Only the usual one for our files, sir.'

'Have it destroyed, and make an official announcement that the visit will take place a few days later than expected. Barricade off the area. No one except our men will be allowed inside. Anyone found damaging the area will be shot on sight.'

'Yes, sir.'

'How many went out on the Transport last night?'

'Nine hundred and sixty.'

'How many are left?'

'Fifty thousand two hundred and seventeen.'

'We must prepare another Transport before the visit.'

'There is a train in Dresden, sir . . . '

'Then order it here immediately.'

'It's bringing more people.'

'More people? Where from? What in hell do they think we are, a goddamn rest camp?'

'It's coming from Poland.'

'A rest camp for the whole of Europe's Jews. Every bloody country in Europe. They're all here. A Catholic priest too. Imagine that. A Jew turned Catholic priest. My mother would turn in her grave.'

'These are Polish *children*, sir, and orders are to isolate them on arrival.'

23

A low, pale moon hung over Terezin. And out of the silence of the night came the sound of the slow puffing of a train.

And then the alarm bell. People were used to hearing the alarm bell at odd hours of the day and night. It was rung whenever a Transport was arriving, an execution taking place or some new restriction being inflicted.

But there was hardly a person in the place whose stomach was not curdled by it.

In the boys' residence at L 365, Jiri sat up and banged his head on the bunk above. Most of the other boys were already pulling on boots.

'Wonder what time it is?' said someone sleepily.

'About three by the look of the moon,' said Jan.

'How in Christ's name can anyone tell without a watch!' said Bedrich.

Young Karel slipped his hand into a slit in the canvas of his straw mattress and pulled out Antonin's watch. He slipped it back in again. It read 2.43. He was too young to resist telling them. But he did resist. It took a lot of will power to keep his mouth shut.

In M 32, Vera had all her girls dress, and then made them lie down to try to sleep again.

'It's probably nothing. And in any case it's not worth worrying about. There's nothing we can do.'

In the grey darkness of the attic she could see the eyes of the girls glistening. They wouldn't sleep. They wouldn't stop worrying. But they would keep quiet and not panic.

Antonin heard the alarm bell too. But he had no idea what it was. So he turned over, cursed the boy who stole his watch, and went to sleep again.

In minutes it came. There were loud-speakers on the corner of every block. No one missed it.

'*Achtung! Achtung!* No one will come into the street. It is forbidden to look from the windows. Anyone found breaking these regulations will be shot. At the second alarm bell these regulations will be in effect. That is in one minute from now.'

'My God,' thought Vera, 'will there ever be a time when they make a mistake – just a single second.'

She counted off the seconds.

They made no mistake.

Except that no one obeyed the regulations. Each window, shuttered or covered with blackout curtain, had a face at it. An appointed face. The eyes of the camp.

They saw it first over on the south-west side of Terezin, because that was where the railway siding came in. On the east side of 'A' street, where it began. The siding ran the whole length of a block. Opposite was the Schlojska.

The train backed through the gate. At the second floor window of A 2, Robicek, a portly middle aged man who worked in the food stores, told the story.

'Five wagons,' he whispered back to his comrades, 'two of them open.'

'What's in them?'

'Wait! I can't see yet. They'll be in the moonlight in a minute.'

'Is it food?'

'It could be. Certainly nothing's moving inside the open cars.'

'Maybe . . . if we made a dash we might get . . .'

Robicek let his eyes roam up the street. SS guards blocked both ends, and at least fifty of them with their machine guns under their arms strutted up and down the street.

' . . . if we made a dash for it . . .' Robicek had a touch of the dramatic in him and he liked to draw things out. ' . . . *if* we made a dash for it . . . we'd all be killed. The street is full of Nazis.'

There was a pause.

'Come on! What's happening?'

'Wait.'

Robicek turned, dropping back the blackout quickly. He stood for a second in silence. The eyes of eighty men were on him.

'Jesus-Maria, it's children!' he said. 'And some of them aren't even dressed!'

Out in the street the guards had opened the brown double gates on the sides of the open box cars. A board with struts across it like a ladder was put up against the opening in the sides of each car. These boards were already worn by the feet of the thousands who had left on the Transports.

At the covered wagons, an officer called an orderly with a crowbar. The man inserted it under the seal. He paused to let the officer take down the number on the seal and then he broke it. Some started pulling back the sliding doors of the covered wagons.

As yet no one had come out. The officer climbed inside the first wagon. He held up a lantern. The light revealed the hollow eyes of about twenty children. They sat, wide awake but almost completely motionless. Some were in a sort of loose pyjama. Others wore jackets and trousers belonging to their fathers. Yet others wore old Polish army uniforms. But they didn't move.

The officer was about to shout 'Stand!' It was the usual command. But he couldn't.

'Where are we, sir?'

The officer looked down. A small boy in pyjamas was looking at him. He brought the lantern down to his level. The boy closed his eyes until they vanished between his cheek bones and his lashes.

'Where are we, sir?' the boy repeated.

The officer swung the lantern. A boy was lying on his back beside the one who spoke. He turned his head slowly to the officer. The chill breath of death came from his mouth.

The officer stood up abruptly.

'You are at Terezin. Your new home.'

'Is it the end, sir?'

'The end? The end of what? You are going to stay here. What's your name?'

'Samuel, sir.'

'Well, Samuel, we've prepared a special barrack for you, and some food. Then you can all go to sleep.'

The officer stood up. He gave an order to have the car cleared. A corporal and two men came up the ramp. The officer handed over the lantern. The corporal started to read from a typewritten order that had been handed to him.

'You have arrived at your new home. We have set up accommodation for you. . . . ' As the officer made his way down the ramp to the street he almost smiled. It was as monotonous and meaningless as a policeman giving evidence in court.

' . . . you will not speak to other prisoners. You will be beaten if you speak to anyone outside your barrack. This is strictly forbidden.'

The officer was now mercifully out of earshot and he was watching the children being brought off the other wagons. Some of them were too weak to walk and they were carried on the backs of their companions. Others were helped by the soldiers themselves. A few refused help and climbed down themselves. Some didn't move from the bottom of the open box cars and their bodies were dragged to one corner out of the way of the feet of their former comrades.

Small carts on wheels, used to carry prisoners' belongings to the Transport, had been ordered forward by the officer.

The very sick were placed in them.

When all were out on the roadway beside the train, lined up ready to move, their shaven heads under the lights from the lanterns looked like brown molehills in a grey field.

No more than seventy had survived the journey from Dresden. Of these perhaps another twenty would die. The rest looked remarkably fit, but weak from lack of food.

As they began to troop off, crossing the tracks behind the train and winding their way down the hill to the barbed-wire fence which had been thrown up around the former soldiers' recreation hut, the man Robicek, at window A 2, said, 'Jesus Christ! They're in terrible condition!'

From behind him he heard someone shout, 'Who are they? Where are they from?'

'Christ only knows,' said Robicek. 'They're not Czechs.'

'How can you tell?'

'I dunno. But they're not.'

'*Lemme* have a look!'

'Don't be a bloody fool!' said Robicek. 'If I can't tell, none of you can.' He pushed the man back on to his bed.

'Maybe they're Ruskies.'

'Maybe, maybe,' Robicek was pulling the old blanket back over his head. 'All I know is that we think we're having it tough here. But those kids have been through hell. *Hell.*'

Robicek knew now what was worrying him. Apart from the voices of the soldiers, there hadn't been another sound outside in the street. Not one of the children had spoken a word.

Down on the railway tracks in the middle of 'A' street, the officer was thinking the same thing as he watched the column wend its way slowly to the barracks.

He was standing akimbo, with his baton behind him. He slapped it across his thigh. There must be something wrong, he was thinking. There is only so much you can take. And then suddenly you come up against a reality which thrusts itself through the tangled web of lies and conditioning. Like a razor. He turned and walked quickly to his room at headquarters.

The first snow of the season fell that night. And within half an hour the train had pulled away and a white blanket covered its tracks.

24

The barrack chosen for the Polish children was in complete isolation from the rest of the camp. In fact it could only be seen by those passing by to the football ground or to the morgue.

It was not heated, of course, but it was warmer inside than out in the December air. And now soldiers were nailing boards to the outside of the windows, covering them completely. This would make it even warmer. An oil drum, half filled with soup, and a crudely carved wooden ladle stood at one end. Most of the children were too weak or too tired to drink. They curled up on the floor, huddling for warmth.

At the far end of the hut was another door. It was locked. All furniture had been removed, the ping-pong table, the bar and its stools, the pin-ups. But the room still stank with the stale smell of spilled beer.

Almost as soon as the last child had been herded into the room, the door was bolted on the outside and a soldier with a machine gun posted there.

It had been an order directly from the Lagerkommandant himself that this was to be carried out.

Dogs were tied to the barbed-wire corners of the fence that surrounded the hut. There was to be absolutely no contact with the rest of Terezin. Anyone approaching the barbed wire or shouting over it at the children was to be shot.

Why this was, no one knew. At this point, not even Bürger himself.

The moon had gone now. Falling snow covered it. The hut was still. But if you looked long enough, you could still make out the shaven heads in the darkness. Especially if you had been used to living in darkness for months. Then darkness became light.

The hut was warmer now and the linoleum on the floor, even though it bore the heelmarks of the soldiers' boots, was luxurious. A few boys – or perhaps they were girls – it was

83

difficult to tell since all had shaven heads – crawled towards the soup drum. They drank hurriedly and greedily. The marrow in their bones was beginning to thaw.

Someone by the door, who had drunk the soup as soon as he saw it, was bringing up. Too much, too soon. But there was no one to tell them that.

Instead someone began to sing.

Holy, holy, holy,
Lord God of Hosts,
Heaven and earth are filled
With your Glory.
Hosanna in the Highest.
Hosanna in the Highest!

It was Samuel and he wasn't singing to thank God he was still alive. He was a far more sophisticated child than that. He sang because he felt like singing.

When he had finished, he ate some lukewarm soup.

25

'I demand to be returned to Prague immediately!' Antonin thumped his left fist into his right palm.

The Lagerkommandant did not change the expression on his face. The two blue almonds merely flickered occasionally.

'My papers, please. At once. My papers!' Antonin was screaming.

The Lagerkommandant coughed, but he did not take his eyes off Antonin. There were witnesses. Vera Lydrakova for one. And the sergeant of the guard in charge of Antonin for another.

'The Red Cross visit is postponed. It is useless for me to stay here.'

'If you continue to shout like a madman I shall have to treat you like one.'

There was a pause. Antonin had tried to control himself, but when the news had come over the loudspeakers that the visit was postponed he had forced his way into the Lagerkommandant's office. He had with him his violin and his make-up. They were on the small chair beside him with his hat on the top.

The Lagerkommandant would have thrown him out ten minutes ago, which was exactly a minute after his unannounced arrival, but he was worried. Berlin was worried too. Certain rumours about the camps in eastern Poland had got about. It gave the Third Reich an unsavoury image abroad, and worse, it had got home, where morale was low. Something had to be done to squelch this image. More so. It had to be rolled flat under a concrete bed for ever.

Terezin, the model Jewish State, the typical example of the Führer's concern for the Jews, had been chosen as the concrete bed on which world opinion would grow and change favourably, like wild violets coming up through the cracks in the concrete itself.

Terezin. It was the centre of too much interest. Bürger had

never met Goebbels, or Eichmann either. He had, of course, met Himmler. But the other men moved in other circles, circles he was afraid of.

Terezin revolted him just as his sickly wife revolted him. It was painful for him to be near it. And now, dangerous.

That was why he had called in Vera Lydrakova to join the angry Antonin. He wanted witnesses for everything. After all Berlin was playing games. The Red Cross visit was obviously to be a real surprise visit after all, and this bloody fool of a comedian was a pain in the arse.

'When is the visit to take place then . . . ?' Antonin had kept up a steady flow of demands and accusations.

'That is none of your business.'

'But I have a right. . . . '

'You have no rights. None whatsoever, except what I choose to grant you.'

'I shall see to it that you are . . . '

The Lagerkommandant sprang to his feet, 'Oh, shut up, man!' The shout stopped Antonin in his tracks. He looked at Vera. She looked down. Could it be that she did not approve? Could it be that she wished him to give up his work outside to remain here to entertain? That was asking a bit much. Certainly he had agreed to entertain. He had realised the need here. But that was before they cancelled the Red Cross visit (for surly it *was* cancelled). And besides there was this refusal to let him have his papers. And the man's attitude. After all Antonin was no ordinary man of the street. He was someone in the theatre and some differentiation ought to be made.

He looked at Vera again. 'I'm sorry, but you do understand? I have commitments.'

'Commitments!' The Lagerkommandant swung round from the window. 'Commitments! You haven't a goddamn commitment in the next year. You're all washed up. I have it all in the files. You're so bad that all the circuits in the country won't have you.' He leant over his desk and pulled out a file. 'Want to read it? It's all in here. All of it.'

Bürger held Antonin's eyes until they fell to his hat on the chair. Antonin dared not look up at Vera.

Bürger usually felt rotten after a fit of emotion. It was unbecoming. But today it made him feel on form.

The truth about yourself in front of someone you have tried to impress always disarms you. Antonin was disarmed.

It was Vera who came to his rescue, 'I don't believe a word

of what they say. There's probably nothing in that file but lies. And everyone in Terezin knows of Mr Karas and his work.'

The Lagerkommandant shrugged, 'Have it your own way.'

Antonin was pleading now, 'Please, sir, give me my papers and let me go. I will sign a document saying I will reveal nothing of what I've seen and then . . . the papers?'

The Lagerkommandant motioned to the sentries, 'Take him away!'

Antonin felt their arms like steel under his armpits.

'But you gave me your word . . . as a German officer and a gentleman!'

'So? Take him away! You may leave, Sergeant. See he's locked in.'

Antonin's hat had fallen on the floor. Vera picked it up and took hold of the violin case handle.

'You gave me your word!' Antonin was twisting round in the doorway and shouting at the top of his voice.

'To you? A Jew?' The Lagerkommandant sat down and started to look again at the papers on his desk. 'Fräulein Lydra-kova you may go. That is unless you'd care for a glass of sherry?'

'Sherry? Yes. I'll take a glass of sherry, Herr Kommandant.'

He swivelled in his chair and pulled open a cabinet behind him. While he was pouring the sherry he was smiling. Vera's eyes were on him. She sat without taking them off his face.

'Prossit!'

'Na zdravi!'

She sipped the sherry and then quickly drained the glass. Through it she could see his stupid smile, like watching a fish in a tank, all wavy and blurred.

She stood up. Taking the glass she smashed it against the wall, and before the smile had time to leave his lips, she walked from the room and slammed the door.

The sherry made her feel good, and besides it was not in her character to waste it.

26

About an hour later that morning, Dr Ernst Hertzog, the chairman of the Elders of the Jewish State of Terezin, came to call on the Lagerkommandant.

Dr Hertzog was short, stocky and in his seventies. He did not like his job, but then he also did not like the idea of someone else doing it. He had great confidence in his own wisdom, and this confidence was borne out by actions which were not too displeasing to the people.

He had been a professor of engineering at Berne, and life was to him a properly balanced wheel.

When Hertzog came to see Bürger there was always some trouble brewing. His first question to him was direct.

'What's the problem now? Can you do nothing by yourselves? Why do you always bring problems to me?'

'It is a matter of advice, Herr Kommandant.'

'On what subject?' It was near lunch.

'The subject of the children who arrived last night, sir.'

'Children? You have been in contact with them?'

'No, sir. But naturally one heard that they had arrived.'

'No one is to have contact with those children.'

'We have gathered together some food and clothing . . . collected voluntarily . . . from the people, for them. I would like it delivered.'

'It shall be.'

'Also one of our doctors, Dr Eric Weinberg, himself a German citizen, has asked him if he may be allowed to treat the children?'

'Weinberg is no German. He's a Jew. And I assure you the children will receive medical treatment. Now anything else?'

Hertzog was rubbing his hands as if washing them. There was obviously something else.

'We wish, respectfully, to know why they are being isolated.'

There was a pause.

'I don't know. Orders from Berlin. Probably in case of typhoid or something.' It was true. Bürger did not know.

'You will see about Dr Weinberg and a nurse, perhaps?'

'I will see. You may go.'

After Dr Hertzog had left, Bürger smoked a cigar. Things were beginning to turn over in his brain. Suddenly he couldn't understand why he'd been so worried.

Someone had to look after the children. Even if it was to feed them and to carry out their dead. Once inside the hut that person would never leave it alive. Thus there would be no evidence.

Bürger pulled on his cigar. He wondered what Hilda, his daughter had for lunch. She had become a very pretty girl. They bathed naked together in the summer months in the pool. She was like his wife, with all the bad qualities hammered from her.

Suddenly he pressed the bell on his desk. His secretary came in, followed by his aide.

'This is an order. Dr Weinberg is to be billeted from henceforth with the Polish children. He is never to leave the building. He is to be accompanied by the clown, Herr Karas.'

He paused. He was killing two birds with one stone. Karas was not officially a prisoner. If he returned to Prague, by some mischance, he posed a dangerous threat. In this way he could never return.

'And accompanying the clown, to look after the female children will be Fräulein Vera Lydrakova.'

He smiled. That would put an end to the tantrums of that skinny bitch. She had broken one of his best Czech crystal glasses that morning. And there was plenty of other Jewish meat around when he wanted to play.

'Food will be taken to the children and placed outside the door. It will be the responsibility of Karas, Lydrakova and Weinberg to collect it. It is repeated that no one will leave that hut.' He stopped and butted out his cigar. 'It is signed by me personally and I want the order carried out within the half hour.'

When the aide and secretary had left, Bürger opened the right-hand drawer of his desk. He took out the identity papers belonging to Antonin and, pulling the waste basket nearer to him, he burned them in it.

'And then, there were none,' he said to himself.

27

When they came to collect Antonin to take him to the barrack where the Polish children were kept, he was lying on his mattress kicking himself for his performance that morning. It had cost him his last possessions. The violin and his make-up. Also his hat.

For the last half an hour there had been a strange banging in the room above him. It was as if someone was kicking the wall with a boot, methodically, almost like the wind banging a shutter.

The two SS men who came for him said nothing. Antonin decided that he would do whatever they asked. He was not ready yet for further protests.

The man who had been sent to collect Vera was bringing her down 'Q' street when Antonin turned the corner to cross the sunken rail tracks. He didn't recognise the other man who followed, also with a guard.

The three met outside the hut. They had no time to say anything to each other. The door was opened and they were pushed inside. Antonin did notice that Vera had his violin, and the other man had a small black bag. That was all. The door slammed behind them.

Back at the SS building where Antonin had been kept, someone walked into the room above, and found the German officer who had supervised the unloading of the Polish children from the train. He was hanging from the light cord. He had been dead several hours, and his feet were banging against the wall.

28

Although it was after midday most of the children were still asleep. As soon as they saw the three visitors they dragged themselves to their feet.

Dr Weinberg, a man in his early thirties, neat, precise and with a medicinal way of looking at you, introduced himself to Antonin and Vera in Czech. He shook hands warmly with Antonin and he bent to kiss Vera's hand. The formalities over, he proceeded to walk down through the crowd of standing children and count heads. The man was obviously an organiser.

Some of the children could not stand; they sat and stared. Antonin looked at Vera.

'You do not wish to talk to me?'

Vera looked at him quickly, then took the hand of a small girl and patted it.

'I'm sorry about this morning. I was out of my mind,' he said.

'I accept your apology.'

'No. I really mean it.'

'Does your career mean so much to you when you are confronted with all of – this!'

'Please do not be angry.'

'Angry? I'm not angry.'

'You certainly look it.'

'I'm disappointed. I had taken you for someone else.'

'What can I say?' He looked at her again but she was talking to a child.

He bent over with her, trying to get her attention.

'I suppose they've sent us here as a sort of temporary punishment. If I caused it. . . . '

'You didn't cause it, now there is work to do. . . . '

'Thank you for bringing my violin.'

The doctor was back at their sides now.

'There are seventy-eight of them. They all need food and a good wash. The food should be here shortly.' He looked at his watch. 'They apparently come from Poland. But they understand German.'

Antonin took a step down the hut. Polish? How well could he remember it? It was spoken by his mother who came from the Tatra mountains, near the Polish border.

'There's no need to stand up. All of you sit down. Lie down if you like,' the doctor said, continuing in his medical manner. But the children didn't seem to understand.

'Can you all hear me?' Antonin said in Polish. 'Sit down. I'm a friend. We are going to get you food . . . it will be coming soon.' He had wandered to the centre of the hut. 'You all know about food . . . don't you?' He paused. . . . 'Like this?'

He put his hand into his pocket and pulled out an imaginary banana. He held it up for all to see. His eyes rolled and he licked his lips with his tongue. Then he elaborately peeled the banana on three sides.

He licked it. There was some laughter and the children began to sit down.

'What's your name?'

Pause.

'You can whisper it if you don't want the others to know!' This brought more laughter. But the boy spoke up plainly.

'My name is Samuel.'

'Samuel what?'

'Samuel. I do not know. I forget.'

'You understand me though?'

'Yes.'

There was another laugh. Maybe it was his Polish that was making them laugh as much as the mime.

Antonin licked the side of the banana again. Then he pretended to try to peel the last quarter. It wouldn't peel. His eyebrows rose and he scratched the top of his head.

He could feel the eyes on him now. He hadn't felt so good in ages. The stench around him was overpowering, but the thin faces broke into smiles that showed swollen gums, yellowed with malnutrition.

He put the banana under his right shoe and tried to pull off the last piece of peel. It wouldn't come. He huffed and he puffed and the children laughed.

At one point he caught sight of Vera. She was looking at him strangely, a slight smile on her lips. But the banana was the important thing. He must concentrate on peeling it.

Suddenly it jumped from under his shoe and into the air. It hit the ceiling and bounced down into his hand.

Some of the laughter was bringing on coughing. The doctor was motioning him to take it easy.

Antonin held the banana tight in both hands. He made one last attempt to get the peel off. Then he let his shoulders droop and he looked at it this way and that. Finally he tossed it to Samuel who caught it neatly.

'Here you try. I can't get the damn thing peeled!' he said. And from then on he always addressed the children in Polish. He strode back up the hut to Vera. The children were clapping their hands with joy.

The doctor was kneeling beside one of the sick children.

'You see, that's all I know. It's all I've ever known about life, and when someone comes and takes that away, I panic.' Vera was listening now. She nodded.

'Will you accept my apologies?'

'Of course.' She smiled and took his hand. He began to feel a warmth coming back into his own body.

The door opened revealing an SS man, his machine gun pointing towards two large carts on wooden wheels outside in the snow. One was filled with clothing. The other with food.

It took Vera and Antonin all their combined strength to get the carts to the door and unload them. Hot potatoes and brown bread. Soup and fresh water. Someone had donated the most precious items of all. Cups made from empty condensed milk tins.

The three adults had to feed the children twelve at a time, because of the number of the cups.

'Do you really not remember your last name?' Antonin asked Samuel.

The boy was fair and blue-eyed. He was very thin and his eyes seemed to burn out of his head as if they were giving out light. His arms were little more than bone, but Antonin had the notion that he had never been a fat boy.

Finally Samuel replied, 'My father, they called him the "Big-one". I don't know why. After they took him away, my sister and I went to the home. We grew up there. We were given the name, Jakob. When they took us to the Jewish camp I kept that name.' The children were beginning to talk again now and there was quite a noise.

'My name is Antonin.'

93

'You are a clown, aren't you?'

'Yes. And very famous too,' Antonin said in mock serious-
ness.

'What is going to happen to us?'

'Nothing. Eat and then we'll see.'

As Antonin rose from his talk with Samuel the door opened
again and Bürger marched in, followed by two aides.

The children sprang up and shrank back against the wall.
Soup and food were spilled.

'I am Lagerkommandant Bürger. I've come to look after
your welfare, and it is I who have sent these people to help you.
You are lucky. You may even have a few laughs. This man here
is a clown.'

Antonin motioned the children to sit again, but they were
once more silent.

Bürger stopped suddenly and looked around the crowd.
Antonin could smell brandy and perfume too. He must have
enjoyed his lunch.

'Is that all you came to say?' said Antonin.

'I beg your pardon. Who do you think you are . . . ?'

'I merely asked you if that's all you came to say.'

'No. As a matter of fact it isn't.' He turned to the crowd
again. 'As you know no one is allowed out of his compound
area,' he pointed to the barbed-wire perimeter around the hut.
'Anyone found outside will be shot. And that goes for you three
too.'

'You mean I've left my girls for good?' asked Vera.

'Yes, dear. The connection is permanently broken. Snapped
– like a sherry glass.' He laughed. 'That's a joke, you see. . . .'

'I understand.' Vera's voice was a razor.

'And I will be leaving when the Red Cross visit is over?'

'You, Herr Karas will be leaving. In two weeks. With all the
children. On a Transport for the East.'

Antonin looked at him. It was no joke this time. His mind
stood still.

'Well, and how do you feel about that?'

Antonin came to life. His fingers regained feeling and his
brain was clear. He said, 'I will go willingly wherever you send
the children. I shall refuse to leave them.'

Bürger's face showed its shock. It was not the answer he'd
expected.

'I mean it, Herr Kommandant, I've found my home. It is here.'

He didn't want to look at Vera, for it was not for her that he had done it. It was for himself. A totally selfish act. This was to be his life. For as long as it lasted.

29

'We must get them washed quickly. They are in a terrible state. It's taken them almost a week to come from Dresden.' It was the doctor speaking and he was holding a key in his hand. 'After that we'll see how many of them we can save . . . I don't know *how* many . . . or really what we're saving them for!'

They had moved all the empty cups and tins to the corner of the room by the door. The doctor walked down the lines of children to the door at the other end. As he passed by the children stood up.

He had opened the lock on the door. He now held the door with his hand and said, 'I want all girls first. Will all the girls come to the front.'

There was a shuffling about of bodies. Vera came down to him with her hands full of clean clothing. She placed it on the linoleum outside the door. There were apparently nearly twenty girls on their feet.

'All right,' said the doctor, 'when I open the door, march in single file and wash. Miss Lydrakova will be with you.'

He flung back the door and the girls started to march in. As the last girl entered there was a scream. It was topped by another scream, and scream upon scream. Antonin ran to the end of the room. Vera forced her way inside the bathroom. The girls were cowering in a corner. They were pointing at the ceiling to where several showers had been placed.

'Gas!'

'Gas! Gas! Gas!' They screamed and began to run backwards from the room as if the showers themselves were following them.

At the word 'Gas', the boys started to run for the locked door at the other end of the room. They climbed up the windows and battered on the woodwork.

'What do they mean – gas?' Vera shouted in Antonin's ear.

'It's all right . . . washing . . . washing.' Antonin was rubbing his hands together and soaping himself.

The girls, most of them nude, continued to scream and call out 'Gas!'

The doctor was running among them trying to pull them from the windows. Vera held a seven-year-old in her arms.

Antonin could think of nothing to stop them until he caught sight of Samuel.

Samuel was not panicking. At least he was not showing it. Antonin went over and took his hand.

At the washroom door, he let go and motioned Samuel to stand there. He turned and blew a trumpet sound through his clenched fists.

Slowly the panic subsided. Occasional deep-throated sobs broke the air.

'Look, boys and girls, this is just washing. You will see.'

He propped the door open with some of the rags that the girls had taken off, and went under a shower.

'No. No. No!' they screamed again. But Samuel stayed firm. Antonin winked at him. A piece of soap lay just inside the washroom near Samuel's feet.

'Throw me the soap, Samuel,' he said in his best Polish.

Samuel bent down and threw it. As he caught it, Antonin turned the shower on. He was fully dressed and the water was like ice.

The children hardly had time to realise. 'Come on, Samuel,' Antonin called.

Without hesitation Samuel came to him under the shower. Antonin began to play now. The crowded faces round the door were relaxing. Antonin gave Samuel the soap and he pretended he also had a bar. Of course he dropped it, and he threw it and he slipped on it, and soon the washroom was full of children, copying him and laughing.

He decided that he had had enough and he elbowed his way through to Vera who stood outside the washroom door.

'That was close. I thought they were going to claw each other to death,' she shouted at him.

'That's what they all thought,' said the doctor.

'What do you mean?' asked Antonin.

'They are from Poland. They've heard some of the rumours . . . perhaps more than *heard* rumours . . . perhaps they've seen it.'

'You mean gas in the showers?'

'That's what they say. But it's only a rumour.'

'My God.' Vera was crying now.

The noise in the washroom was deafening. Antonin took Vera by the arm and led her to the other end of the room. Children were running in and out of the ice-cold water and the doctor was scolding them and telling them to get dressed in the new clothing, and they were paying no attention.

Vera had stopped crying now. All her tears were stifled inside.

'You're all wet. You'd better get some dry clothing,' she said.

'Hope there's something to fit me.'

'There's something to fit everyone, Mr Karas,' said Vera searching through the heap.

'Please call me Toni and I'll call you Vera,' he said quickly.

Vera kept her head down searching. 'All right,' she said in a voice that sounded busy.

At last Vera came up with a shirt. Antonin took off his jacket and shirt and put the dry one on. Then he put the wet jacket back on again. 'It will dry quicker that way,' he said.

'I'm afraid there aren't any pants big enough.'

'Never mind. . . .'

'Wait a second. Try these.' She held a pair up against him. 'You know, you're going to help us a lot. It means a lot to laugh.'

'That's my line of business.'

'No, they're too small, you'll have to dry your own.'

'Vera?'

'Yes?'

'I'm happy. And I haven't been happy for some time.'

'You might just as well be happy. Being angry won't help.'

'I know now.' Antonin unbuttoned his trousers and wrung them out.

The doctor came running over. 'For God's sake give us a hand. There's pandemonium in there. You'd think it was a school picnic. I can't get them out and the water's freezing me!'

Vera and Antonin followed him down the hut to the showers.

30

'I don't know about you two, but I'm hungry!' said Antonin.

It was evening. And inside the hut the blankets which had been provided by the Jewish Elders of the State of Terezin were covering the children, who seemingly without exception slept soundly.

The doctor expected little more trouble. Seven children had died during the day. The remainder he hoped with food and a prayer might come through.

Vera was absolutely exhausted. Her bones ached pleasantly and her head swam with thoughts and impressions that would remain with her until the end. The end? Bürger had boasted of two weeks. This, she knew, was just a threat. Anything could happen. Especially with the Red Cross coming. The war might even come to an end. Tonight, she didn't really care what happened, although she'd have liked to get Antonin some food.

Thin chinks of moonlight filtered through the boarding the men had put over the windows. Fingers of blue, they hit the faces of the children. It was like a benediction.

Vera's father was Jewish, but her mother was Catholic. She had never been inside a synagogue, although her religion had been always registered as Jewish. Occasionally as a small girl she had been taken to the church run by the nuns at Loreta Abbey up near Prague Castle. Here, surrounded by the Baroque statues and high gilt windows, she had indulged her senses in what she supposed was religion. The incense from the high, white and ormolu altar, the smell of candlewax and the mustiness of the rough benches swept into her senses still. The Latin, which the priest mumbled quickly, and the sermon, which he stumbled through, meant nothing. But the smell of wet clothing, drying from the snow, the stomping of heavy boots on the floor and the almost incessant coughing, had stayed with her.

It was the place she had last seen her mother. They had

waited for her outside the church with the truck to take her to the Transport. Her crime was apparently marrying a Jew. It was the place she too had last visited when she knew that she and her whole class were to be transported that afternoon. The processing point in Prague on Veletrzni, near Hermanova was a temporary wooden building. The railway ran beside it.

In actual fact there had been no need for her to go. She had volunteered because all her children were to be sent.

By the time she reached Terezin she heard her mother had died of typhoid, which swept the camp in the early days.

But that was all in the past, and the past meant nothing.

Today, she was seated on the floor of this over-crowded, but apparently luxurious hut, beside this strange, thin man who could make children laugh and was yet so unhappy himself. His ego aggravated her. His pettiness was worse than the worst of her children. His vanity made her laugh. And he was so easily hurt. But he gave of himself, and that was good.

You tended to categorise people in a concentration camp. Characteristics, good and bad, stuck out of each man's face, now that the mask of society had been taken away. There was no attempt to hide. And at first sight she had liked Antonin. He was bright, almost cheeky, and refreshing. But later she'd come to see the cowardice in him and the pride. Today had made her change her opinion again. So that now she was not sure. There was more to see in this man. More to hear about his thoughts.

Like all women she was curious and she felt the urge to give herself to finding out. And that was both a good and a bad sign.

'Won't they bring us any food?'

The doctor was asleep now, his head resting on his chest and his arms folded. The gold band of his wedding ring was catching one of the beams from the wooden windows.

'I doubt it,' Vera whispered. 'We could try banging on the door. I can hear a man outside.'

'I can't hear a thing.'

'You get used to listening carefully.'

'The doctor deserves his sleep,' said Antonin glancing at him. 'That wedding band reminds me of the one on the finger of Bürger's secretary.'

'It does look like it. I'm surprised he still has it. It must be gold.'

'The band is too big on Bürger's secretary.'

'It was a present from Bürger.'

'A present?'

'He cut it off the finger of a dead woman and gave it to her when she married one of his men.'

The thought stayed with Antonin for a while.

'There's no way to break the system, is there?'

'None.'

'There must be some way. We can't just accept what they do.'

'It's too late now.'

'I suppose so.' Antonin felt automatically in his pocket for a cigarette. A cigarette would be good now. But there wasn't even any loose tobacco. 'Do you suppose if we knocked softly, he might open the door and ask someone to get some food?'

'He could be shot for it.'

'It wouldn't hurt to ask. He'd be too scared to harm us after what Bürger said.'

Vera rose to her knees and put her ear to the door.

'He's leaning against it. I can hear him breathing. Let me try.'

Her knuckles on the door were like piano hammers. They waited a fraction of a second and they heard the door being unlocked. It opened a chink letting in brilliant moonlight reflected on the snow.

Vera spoke in perfect German. 'Is it cold out there?'

'My feet are ice.'

'How long is your duty?'

'I'm not allowed to say.'

Antonin saw Vera slip her hand through the door and touch the man's hand. 'You *are* cold!'

For some reason it made Antonin angry. Perhaps it was the tone of her voice.

'Perhaps later on, if it gets worse, we'll take those boots off and rub your feet.'

'That would be good.'

Vera's hand was still in the man's and Antonin could see her face smiling up at him. 'Listen,' she said, 'we've had nothing to eat today, can you get a message to Robicek in A 2?'

'That would be impossible.'

'Isn't anyone around?'

'Just Stein. His job's to patrol from here to the Schlojska.'

'What's he like?'

'He's a Hamburger!'

Both Vera and the man laughed.

'Then it should be easy.'

'I don't think I could do it.'

'I'll give you something for it. Later on.'

'No. I don't think so. . . . '

There was a pause.

'All right, I'll do it. And I don't want anything for it. I'll just do it, understand.' And the door closed and was locked again quickly.

'There, see. Everything is possible. Soon you will have something to eat.'

Antonin did not look at her.

'What's the matter, are you angry again?'

'I don't want the food.'

'Sulking?'

'Not at all.'

She laughed. 'You needn't be shocked. It has happened many times, when people are sick and children are hungry. All of us women. And there is usually a way out. Only the biggest pigs will accept you . . . and they will take you anyway.'

Soon there was a soft knock on the door. The unbolting again.

The voice outside said, 'I've a little sausage here and some bread. It's my ration. Take it. When I'm relieved I can go to the cookhouse and feed up.'

The door was shut quietly again and the food was in Vera's hands.

31

The next few days passed quickly. The doctor kept count on a small calendar he had in his black case, and he organised the day in such a way that even the smallest and most sickly child was occupied as much as possible.

Vera and the doctor spoke to the children in German, Antonin in his Polish with the funny Czech accent.

There was no midday meal. The only meal came, as it did throughout Terezin, early in the morning. It was a weak soup made from whatever the cooks happened to have, and some bread made from potato flour. The bread was very precious. Each portion weighed approximately two ounces and the harder it was the better. It lasted longer. For children, eating this meal involved a decision. On the one hand the philosophy was to save the bread and nibble on it as you grew more hungry through the day. In this way you always had something to look forward to. But it needed a lot of will-power. The other philosophy was to eat the bread with the soup. You then felt full for an hour or so, and besides if anything happened to you during the day, at least you'd have enjoyed a meal which no one could steal – not even if you were put on a Transport.

In the hut, the doctor divided the bread into two. So that each child had something in the evening. It was more of a comforter than anything, but it kept them happy.

After midday the children were allowed out into the barbed-wire compound around the hut for recreation. It was a privileged hour, and the doctor had cut the end off a rubber syringe, plastered an adhesive bandage strip on the hole and made a sort of ball.

Girls and boys played together, shouting and laughing, gaining strength with each hour. To Antonin, the change was a miracle. A few, still numbed by the terrors they had experienced, stood beside the wall of the hut and watched, but gradually they too were enticed into the games.

Leap-frog was a favourite. Antonin could never resist taking his place in the line-up to jump over the backs of the bending children. When it came to his turn he always managed to collapse just as he bent over. Invariably he hit his foot on an imaginary stone and nursed an imaginary sore toe. Another favourite was 'tag'. And trying to catch Antonin was like trying to catch a fish. He could twist his body into the most amazing positions so that grabbing hands missed by inches.

One afternoon, after they had been in the hut three days or more, Antonin took some planks that had been left lying in the corner of the compound by the soldiers. He and a dozen or more children dragged them into the centre of the earthen area, where most of the snow had been worn away by the games.

'What are you going to do?' asked Vera.

'We,' said Antonin, 'are going to make a fort.'

'A fort!' Vera was shocked. After all they were living in one.

'Yes, a fort, aren't we, boys?'

The boys began to scream and shout with joy.

'We'll start right here by putting this plank . . . ' Antonin lifted it into place, 'at the bottom.' All the wood had come from some nearby barn and there were a few nails sticking out of it.

Vera and the doctor stood to one side and watched. Soon there was indeed a sort of topless box, about two metres by three, with a gap in one side as a gateway.

'How high shall we make it?' Some of the children were pushing to get inside and Antonin was having to hold them back.

'We'll make it as high as . . . you!' said Antonin, pointing to a small dark boy of about eight. He took the boy and led him into the fort. 'Yes, that's just right.'

The boy peered through the cracks in the boards and shouted to his comrades.

'I got you. I got you!' He wagged his finger and made the noise of a gun with his mouth.

Antonin grinned, 'We're going to play cowboys and Indians. I guess I'll have to be the Indian chief. I don't think there'll be many volunteers for Indians.'

They played during all of that recreation period.

At the end Vera saw Antonin looking seriously at the fort.

'So serious after such a triumph?' she asked.

'I'm thinking how funny it is to be happy at a time like this.'

'What better time is there to be happy?'

He looked at her and he knew then the truth.

32

One evening, after the doctor had made his rounds and the bread had been handed out, the children started to sing.

It was a familiar song with Polish words. Someone had taught it to them, Antonin supposed, when they were at the other camp. The tune was well-known.

Antonin hadn't played his violin since he had been at the camp. It had never occurred to him to open the case again after the old man had stolen the cigarettes, but Vera had put it in a corner of the hut, propped against the wall, and he took it out now and began to play along.

'You brought the violin, but what did you do with my hat?' he asked.

'First I stamped on it. Then I threw it out in the rag collection,' she said.

He laughed. 'You must have been angry.'

'I was. Very.'

He was tuning up now and trying to catch the words.

'Oh well, I needed a new one.'

He began to finger the melody, running his roughened hands up and down the strings as if it were the first time he'd ever played.

He had the words now. They went something like this:

When I get up in the morning,
The leaves are tapping my window.
When I get up in the morning,
The cat is lapping its milk.

The sun is always awake by then
And the swallows have left their nests.
My father's planting corn by then,
And mother's baking bread.

When I get up in the morning,
The grass is wet with dew.
When I get up in the morning,
I wonder what I shall do?'

I've all day to do it in
And haven't a thought in my head.
But by the time it comes to evening
I've done it all and more.

The day's been full and wonderful
And yet as I go to bed,
I wonder what I did?

But when I get up in the morning
I wonder what I shall do?

The children sang the song until they began to drop off to sleep, but the melody lingered in the minds of the three adults until they too were nearly asleep.

Vera opened her eyes and saw a figure moving slowly and carefully towards them.

It was Samuel. She put out her hand and touched Antonin. He too had seen Samuel.

'Sit down. You don't have to stand there.'

An earnest conversation began in Polish. Vera could only catch a few words of it.

'Please, sir. I want to ask you a question.'

'Ask it then, Samuel.'

'Well . . . *er* . . . will you and Miss Lydrakova be here . . . stay with us?'

'We will be staying with you as long as we are allowed.'

'I mean . . . to the end?'

'End? The war's going to be over soon. Then we'll leave you.'

'No. My father told me. . . . '

'What did he tell you?'

'He told me that we must not expect to be free even at the end of the war.'

'Where is he now, your father?'

'They took him to the gas chambers, I think. But he was right.'

'Perhaps he was right. But when the war's over we'll have to make sure we are all free. Make sure all this can't happen again. It'll be up to us, won't it?'

'I suppose so, sir. But . . . well . . . I just wanted to know if you and Miss Lydrakova will be here with us?'

Antonin took his hand and shook it. The boy turned and bowed slightly to Vera. 'Please translate for her. I don't think she understands. I want her to be with us too.'

'I will translate, and now you go back and get some sleep or you'll have me acting the fool and waking everyone up.'

Samuel suppressed a giggle and Antonin led him back to the blanket he was sharing with three other boys.

Later he told Vera. She said, 'It's good to be needed, isn't it?'

'It's essential. I've always thought I was needed by people for only one thing . . . to make them laugh. The rest of me seemed a shell.'

'Even to your wife?'

'You knew I was married?'

'A woman can usually tell.'

'She died a year ago . . . and after that I sort of fell to pieces. . . . '

'I understand.'

There was a pause. He could feel her thigh against his leg. He knew her eyes were on his face. He turned to her and let his face droop into a rubbery mask. She laughed. It was a way out of their embarrassment. '*Ssssh!* You'll wake up the doctor. Listen to him snore.'

'He's a good fellow.'

'He's a brilliant surgeon they say. That's probably why they haven't cut off his ring. After the war he wants to start a clinic in Lausanne.'

'I've got my plans too,' said Antonin. 'A new comedy theatre in Prague.'

'That's the trick to life here . . . to keep having plans.' She laughed again. 'They'll probably change from day to day.' She stopped. 'I'm trying not to think about it, but I wonder what's happening to my girls?'

'They're all right.'

'Luba will take charge.'

'Toni?'

'Yes?'

'I'm glad you're feeling happier.'

'Never been so happy in my life. Best audience I've ever had. I never thought I had the talent and to tell you the truth I always looked down on children's entertainers. Horrible, wasn't it?'

'But you're over that now?'

'Yes.'

There was another silence. He wanted very much to kiss her, but he was embarrassed.

Instead he turned and shook her hand. 'Good night,' he said quickly and shuffled away to a spot reserved for him near Samuel.

Vera lay on her back, hoping to hear him shuffle back beside her. But he never returned.

'When I get up in the morning, I wonder what I shall do? . . . ' she sang to herself.

33

When the SS guard on the door let them out for recreation the next day, the sun was shining and it was quite warm. By the time they had blinked their eyes into focus they were all aware that the sudden heat had melted the snow and left the ground in puddles and wet sandy stretches.

The doctor was handed a slip of official paper. It was an order from Bürger.

It read: WE HAVE HAD YOUR CHILDREN'S FORT REMOVED. WE CANNOT ALLOW THE TEACHING OF WAR-LIKE GAMES FOR CHILDREN. IT IS CONSIDERED HARMFUL. *Signed*, BÜRGER, LAGERKOMMANDANT.

When the doctor showed the order to Antonin and Vera, they laughed.

The children didn't laugh. They were angry, and it took Antonin quite a time to calm them. He let some leap-frog and others amused themselves with tag.

Samuel had got hold of the doctor's improvised ball. During recreation, the guard was always placed outside the barbed-wire fence. In that way messages could not be passed easily, and yet a watch on the children could be kept.

Samuel and a couple of friends were tossing the ball into the air and trying to catch it. When they dropped it, which they often did, it bounced in the most peculiar way, like a soft egg.

Antonin saw it all happen. And even as the ball first landed inside the barbed wire he knew it was going to bounce over the fence.

It did. It landed in a small bush about three metres from the SS guard.

Before Antonin could shout, Samuel said to his friend, 'Stay here, I'll get it!'

He lay on his stomach and began to wriggle under the wire. It was amazing how thin and small he seemed to be. His head was now through on the other side and he was reaching for the ball.

Antonin wanted to shout but he knew this would alert the guard. He ran to the fence. The boy's feet were now outside too, so that Antonin could not pull him back in again. He was thanking God that there was so much noise in the recreation area that the guard had heard nothing at the fence.

By the time Antonin reached the fence and pressed himself against it, feeling the barbed wire cutting into his shirt, Samuel's hand was on the ball.

At that second the guard turned and with one pace put his boot on the boy's hand.

Samuel looked up at the boot and then his eyes went fearfully up to the man's face looking down at him.

It was a new guard, one they had never seen before, and who probably had had his instructions that morning, for the first thing he said was, 'Well, so we're trying to escape, are we?' And he pulled Samuel up by the neck.

'Leave him alone. He's only trying to get the ball.'

'He's trying to escape! What's he doing outside the barbed wire? Why didn't he ask me if he wanted his ball?'

'Let him go. I shall inform the Lagerkommandant,' shouted Antonin.

'That's where he's going. Now. *Lauf!*'

Still holding Samuel by the neck he started out down the road to the main part of the camp.

By this time all the children were standing at the barbed wire.

Antonin shouted, 'You can't do that. He's not allowed out of barracks. You'll get into trouble for letting him get out.'

The man stopped suddenly. He let go of Samuel's short stubby neck. 'I'll get into trouble if I don't,' he shouted back. And he returned to where the ball was still lying. 'This is evidence. I shall need that.' He was now holding Samuel by the arm.

Vera suddenly shouted, 'Don't you have a boy like that somewhere?'

The man paused and wiped the ball on his coat.

'Don't you have a boy? Can't you understand he was just getting the ball?' Vera repeated.

The man looked at her. He tossed the ball in his hand. He looked at Samuel again.

'You'd have him shot down, would you? Bring him back – for the sake of your own son!'

The guard was still tossing the ball. He dropped it. There was a titter of laughter from the children.

Then the guard grinned. 'Here, pick it up and get back in there again. And if I see anyone getting out again, I swear I'll kill him. It's orders. And orders is orders. Now scram.'

Samuel was already half way through the barbed wire and a cheer went up as he was pulled inside by Antonin.

It was a good thing that the guard had decided not to take Samuel to Bürger. Good for both of them. Bürger had just received a very annoying cable.

34

What annoyed Bürger most was that the cable was three days old. Where had it been held up? Or was it backdated to make him look a fool?

He turned it over in his hands as if the back of the message could tell him more.

Meanwhile, his aide stood at attention, and waited.

'Are you sure that no one has touched anything on the green side of the walls?'

'The men have patrolled constantly, and I checked this morning myself.'

'If they are to arrive on Thursday, it gives us only three days.'

'At 1300 hours, sir.'

'Yes, three days and nearly one hour!' He flicked his fingers and Hans, the Alsatian, came and licked his hand. 'I want you to cancel all my appointments this afternoon. We will go over the schedule together. You will bring me the papers after lunch. Oh, and tell Hilda to have my green tweed suit pressed. The Harris. I shall be wearing it. More suitable, I think.'

'The film-making crew has already arrived, sir. They want to know when they can go to work.'

'We will stage some events for them on Thursday morning, but they will shoot nothing before that. They are all German?'

'From Berlin, sir. The Propaganda Ministerium.'

'Christ! Did you ever see a picture of Herr Eichmann?' Bürger tossed a picture from a newspaper clipping across his desk.

'Take a look. With Jews at Belsen!'

'Is he coming?' asked the aide nervously.

'I doubt it.'

He picked up another clipping. 'And this is Sussens. There are two Swedes and a Portuguese coming with him. Do we have any sardines?' He smiled at his own joke.

'And if anyone puts up a banner or hangs himself over the green wall, I'll take severe reprisals.'

'I have arranged for the blocks to the west and north to be cleared, sir. There will be a guard of honour going ahead of the party to clear away any demonstration, but rest assured there will be none.'

'That's what you think. Never trust a Jew. Especially when he's pushed into a corner.'

'I quite agree, sir.' The aide was taking notes while still at attention.

Bürger wanted to light a cigar, but he had no more matches. So he chewed.

'How many wagons are there at our disposal in Prague?'

'Perhaps thirty, sir. I could check.'

'I want fifty. And I want them here at dawn on Wednesday.'

'Fifty, sir?' The aide was very nervous now.

'I said fifty, and an engine big enough to pull them a long way. I want the train staffed by a Kompanie Pioniere. Armed men. A military train.'

'But sir, what for?'

'You'll see. Don't forget my suit and be back at 1400 hours sharp with the schedules.'

'Yes, sir.'

'By the way,' said Bürger as he passed the aide on his way out to his car to take his lunch, 'the banker, the shopkeepers, the people who will walk the streets? They are trustworthy?'

'To the best of my knowledge.'

'At 1400 hours.'

'At 1400 hours, sir.'

35

'The time has come. It's the day after tomorrow,' said Antonin. Vera, who had been standing quietly at the end of the hut waiting for the giggling girls to come out of their daily shower ritual, shivered unconsciously.

'When did you know?'

'That aide of Bürger's just gave me the papers.'

'All of us?'

'Apparently.'

'Where's the doctor?'

'In the washroom treating a cut. Nothing serious.'

The boys who were waiting for their turn in the showers were excitedly chatting about a game they had just played at recreation. They had burst the doctor's football in the process and one boy, Stanislaus, was getting all the blame.

Antonin suddenly could not bear the noise.

'Shut up. Silence everyone!' he shouted at the top of his voice. 'Silence!'

As soon as he had shouted, he wished he hadn't, because the boys were startled and frightened.

'It's all right. Just be a little less noisy.'

Bürger's aide had come with a sergeant of the SS. Antonin had not known it, but the man was the sergeant in charge of all Transports. He had brought with him a list of instructions. The time they were to move out from the hut. The time they were to arrive at the Schlojska, the time of this and that and the other. The list was pages long and included such items as the confiscation of firearms prior to boarding, the weight of the possessions one could carry (not more than twenty-five kilos) and the type of clothing to be worn.

As his eyes scanned the list, Antonin caught sight of one item that made him start to laugh. He had been looking for something to laugh at.

'It says here that if garlic is found on the person of any

prisoner being transported he will be shot!'

To his surprise, Vera took the instruction quite seriously.

'Didn't you know? We are forbidden to eat garlic here. It is as serious as being found smoking.'

'Why garlic?'

'Why smoking?'

'It's all totally mad.'

'Exactly.'

'I suppose it's no good . . . putting up any resistance?'

'It's been tried. It never works. Someone usually does though. But more end up being killed.'

The doctor emerged from the showers, soaking wet, with a small girl crying in his hands. 'They face the worst of disasters without so much as a tear and when it comes to getting a splinter out of a toe there's a howling match.'

He placed the girl on a blanket and wrapped her in it.

'What are you two looking so melancholy about?'

'We are to be Transported. The day after tomorrow.'

The girls had started to stream out of the washroom now and the boys were fighting to get in.

'Hold it! Hold it!' The doctor shouted. 'I want small boys first . . . and then you people here.' He made a big circle with his hands, which he was trying to dry on his shirt. 'And lastly you boys. And no tomfoolery or I'll be in!'

He turned back to Antonin, 'I heard the rumour last night. Robicek came. He has a stolen uniform you know. Looks quite smart in it too. Apparently we aren't the only ones. They've ordered fifty wagons from Prague. The Elders were meeting making up lists when Robicek came. There'll be over three thousand of us.'

'Three thousand!'

'Well, the place was getting rather crowded. After all it will leave about forty-nine thousand here in a place designed for six thousand people. You can't just drop a zero and tell the Red Cross there are only five thousand, besides that wouldn't be German.' He smiled, 'I wouldn't even approve of it myself as a German.'

Antonin looked at him. In spite of his banter there were tears in his eyes. 'Any idea where we are going?'

'Eastern Poland is my guess. It's like heaven. You never know until you get there.'

'It's not going to be easy. How are we going to tell them?'

'Best if we do it as soon as possible. They'll get over the shock here and be calm at the train,' said Vera.

'Yes, but what in the name of Jesus are they going to do with us? Send us to another overcrowded camp?'

'Another overcrowded camp!' the doctor was suddenly enraged. He shook his fist at Antonin. 'You simple idiot!' he was shouting. 'You know those pipes and concrete foundations they are making in the small fortress? Well, they've had those at a camp called Auschwitz for two years. Completed! Completed, I tell you. Jesus Christ, man! When you get off the Transport they divide you into two lines. Young women and working men on one side. Children and the old on the other. They march the women and workers into the camp and the rest go to the bloody showers. They never come out. The population of Auschwitz is never overcrowded. It remains constant!'

He stood there, a fat, square man, the tears rolling down his cheeks, and he blew his nose on his shirt. He was calm now.

'I apologise. But some of us have known for some time. These children know. That's why they isolated them. And with the Red Cross coming on Thursday they want to get rid of anyone who might know.'

He blew his nose again. 'You must excuse me. There's a boy in the showers who is epileptic. I have to watch him.'

'But when,' said Antonin, 'when shall we tell them?'

'When they've all showered and we've given them something to eat.'

36

They told the children half an hour later. It was much easier than Antonin had anticipated. There had been no panic. Not even a tear. The only question asked was from Samuel. He wanted to know where they were being sent. But as no one could answer him, he stayed silent until they were all bedded down. Then he came up to Vera and shook her hand.

'You are both coming?'

'We wouldn't leave you now,' said Antonin.

'I have to know.'

'It's a promise. And who knows it may even be a better place than this.'

'Thank you.' He shook hands again and went back to his blanket.

Later that night there was a tap on the door. Vera was nearby when it opened. A voice said, 'This came in a Red Cross parcel for me today. Several hundreds arrived. I stole five of them.'

The door closed again. In Vera's hands were five Swiss chocolate bars.

Five bars to be divided between sixty-three? It wouldn't go very far, but the gesture was good.

Meanwhile, at SS headquarters, Bürger rose from the desk. He was in his braces. The aide sat stiffly beside him.

'Complete. And timed to the second. We'll have a rehearsal tomorrow and that will be all.'

'And the entertainer, Herr Kommandant?'

'Yes, Karas, and Lydrakova.' Bürger shrugged. 'A problem. We may have a problem on our hands. They will have left by the time the visitors arrive, but we can manage without them. After all, there is no official programme, is there? It's all perfectly unrehearsed? I think the band, the street dancers, the exhibitions of art and the children singing is sufficient display of Jewish talent. We don't want to overdo it, do we!'

'No, sir. Very wise.'

'Well, I'm for bed. Good night. Turn out the lights before you leave.'

He collected his tunic and greatcoat, and left.

37

Dawn came brightly that December morning. The sun rose over the fortress walls, and those inmates of D 246, the only three-storeyed stone building in Terezin, were lucky enough to see it tip the hills to the north-west of the place, and filter itself through the evergreens.

But it was cold. Bitterly cold. There were already over a thousand people in the Schlojska when the children were double-marched in. Old Robicek, from his vantage point overlooking the line had seen the train pull in during the night. There were indeed fifty wagons. The train stretched from the very gate to the end of the line. There were two engines, and the whole ensemble was being run by men from the Kompanie Pioniere – the German Corps of Engineers – who were even now busying themselves with rags and oil cans, trying to make two weary-looking engines into efficiently operating machinery. The grey and the black camouflage gave the train a snake-like head, but it did not extend to the wagons, some of which had been in recent use bringing cattle from Slovakia and the Ukraine.

The Schlojska itself was a tin shed abutting a large two-storey grey stone building which surrounded a huge courtyard. There was nothing inside the Schlojska except air, and as the place filled up with the prisoners, who came in fifties and sixties from each block, there was precious little of that.

As Antonin, Vera, the doctor and the children were herded inside they could hardly see, but when the darkness adjusted their eyes they saw silent uncomplaining faces around them. Then the door slammed and the noise of the guards marshalling the next batches of prisoners was all that was left of Terezin.

It was the strangest feeling. Antonin had hated Terezin. He had seen, in his short stay, every type of brutality and stupidity. Yet, he was troubled at leaving it. It had become a refuge, a warren where you came to understand how to avoid the dangers and to exist. Almost a home.

Many in the Schlojska had left behind, secreted in floor-boards and in the earth, mementos and precious items. Things far above their worldly value. Small irregular pebbles; drawings on cardboard torn from the sides of cases in which officers' liquor arrived; music scribbled on planks and inside book covers. A list of football players pinned to a wall for a match that would never take place. A spoon carved from the bough of an elm. The list was almost endless, for nearly everyone had something.

Then again many had brought things with them. They knew the regulations, of course. The lists had been read and re-read to them. A change of clothing, a ration of bread, a toothbrush and toothpaste. A toothbrush! There might as well be, thought Antonin, a regulation about grand pianos.

He could feel Vera near to him. Her hand accidentally touched his. Or *was* it an accident? He touched back. It wasn't. He looked down. The eyes of young Samuel burned bright in the darkness. The children were silent. An occasional cough or shuffle broke the waiting.

'I suppose it's absolutely no use putting up a fight or something?' he repeated.

Vera shook her head, 'It never works,' she affirmed.

'We've got to do something.'

'Outside there in the courtyard some will try, you will see.'

'But there must be something!'

'Nothing! There is nothing, Toni!'

'D'you know what's wrong?'

'Yes? . . . '

'Do you know, our trouble is that . . . we have all been con-ditioned to accept. As long as we know that. Then surely there must be another way!' said Antonin. 'People are living in a dream.'

'And you aren't?'

Antonin thought hard. 'Perhaps. But I think for me it's been different. I've become awake.'

'Perhaps you have. But what can we do?'

'I dunno. I don't mean start a riot. That would be foolish. But a plan. Quick and well organised . . . something!'

'Please be careful,' she said and took his hand.

'I'm going to think of some way. And it will succeed! Some-how!'

The Schlojska was suddenly flooded with light from the open-ing of a door in the western side. The door led to the archway and into the courtyard. The light startled people and they began to talk nervously, to curse and swear at each other and to accuse each other of pushing, punching and even stealing.

They came through the archway as if it were the highway to freedom, straining and fighting.

At a quick glance, Antonin reckoned there were about eight hundred people already in the courtyard. It was much bigger than he had anticipated and he now understood why the Germans had chosen this building to use as the entraining depot. The eight hundred were lined up in what Antonin assumed were block and street numbers. They stood to attention and faced the walls. Ten deep and about a pace apart. A four metre gap ran through the centre to the other archway. On the other side of that, as everyone knew, was the train. The gate to it was shut.

Beside the archway was a small table. And beside the table, in cardboard boxes, were white cards with numbers on them. Attached to each white card was a piece of string. Just enough to go round a person's neck.

The sun was now hitting the top of the western end of the courtyard. All the windows had been opened on the second storey. At the end, over the western archway, was a fancy double window and a small balcony. Once it had been the reviewing stand for the commanding officer of one of Maria Theresa's garrisons. Now it held a man with a machine gun. Soldiers were posted at most of the windows. If anyone tried anything here, the train would leave loaded with corpses.

'Lauf! Lauf!'

Just for once couldn't they let people walk? thought Antonin. Old and young ran to rearranged positions where soldiers held up cards with street numbers on them. Within minutes they were all in place behind the groups already there.

Vera and Antonin, accompanied by the doctor, were once again isolated. They were 'run' to a corner under the eaves to the south. The snow was still on the cobbles here. Vera was looking round at the children and smiling. But the children just stared ahead. There was something almost funny about all the people being marched into the courtyard, for the next batch from the Schlojska was coming in. They squabbled like a lot of hens and behaved like naughty children. Some women pushed babies in home-made carts. Each clutched a bundle of clothing. One man came on crutches and pointed angrily with one of them at his wife as she struggled along with both their bundles of clothing. Another walked erect, tall and angular, carrying a shooting stick. He didn't run. He marched.

Soon there were nearly two thousand in the courtyard and the air was beginning to warm up. Antonín clutched his violin. It was the sole possession of the group. They had what they stood up in, and four ounces of black bread each. It couldn't be a very long journey. Perhaps they were taking them only to Prague?

The very thought of the tall spires of the city, sitting so peacefully in the valley of green wooded hills, made Antonín excited. He must keep his mind on one thing. Freedom!

The German soldier stood about half a metre in front of him. His machine gun was at the port-arms position and cocked. Antonín tried to reach his eyes, but they went through the group to the grey wall behind.

The eyes were brown, with weather-beaten crinkles. Apart from this his face was a plum. And about eighteen years old. His neck was white, except for a thick red line where the rough collar of his tunic had rubbed.

'What's the poor young bastard thinking?' Antonín asked himself.

Was it pride which made him stand so grimly to attention? Made him polish his buttons on his tunic to sunlight bright? Made him fanatically obedient?

Antonín was interrupted in his thoughts by the sudden silence which fell over the courtyard, followed by the click of boots on cobbles.

Bürger had arrived. He stood with his aide, and two soldiers with machine guns, under the western arch. The Alsatian was at his feet. The last straggling sick from the hospital were being carried in by their fellow prisoners on improvised stretchers.

Except for the walkway down the centre there was hardly another space in the courtyard.

Antonín tilted his head to one side.

'Dr Hertzog's here!' he whispered to Vera. The guard's eyes flickered warningly.

'The Elders are making some substitutions,' she said.

'What substitutions?'

'You will see. Always certain favours are granted at the last minute. It is the Elders' privilege.'

'What favours?'

'*Halt's Maul!*' the guard said quietly.

122

The sergeant who had been sitting at the table writing on long lists, stood up.

The lists were handed to each soldier in charge of a group. The soldier then called the roll.

When it came to Antonin and the children there were only two names on the list. One was Vera Lydrakova, the other the doctor. It was followed by a list of numbers.

It annoyed Antonin that his name was not on it. He could understand about the children because they probably didn't even know their names. But why was his name left off?

He looked about at other groups. Everyone was accounted for, it seemed. He was about to say something, make an objection, but he restrained himself. All his energy would go into making a plan. The success of his life would depend on the success of the plan. Antonin Karas, you fail or become a hero. It is up to you.

The roll call had ended.

'There will be the following substitutions,' the weak old voice of Dr Hertzog was hardly heard down at Antonin's end of the courtyard. Maybe he was going to be substituted? For a fleeting moment his heart held a hope that his head killed.

'Dvorak!' The old man coughed. There was something guilty in the cough.

'Jelinek, Zapotek, Stastna, Stepanek, Capek, Klement, Hermanakova,' he paused again to cough, 'Bederich, Narodni, Hellman, Koch, Pellisier, Montecorvo. . . . '

Antonin, hearing the names of the different nationalities, looked around him again on tip-toes. He could see Italian faces, French faces, Dutch and Danish faces, German faces, Polish faces. He had never realised what an international group they were at Terezin.

As each person's name was called the person ran forward and stood beside the table, in between the Elder and Bürger.

It was now about ten o'clock. They had been standing for over two hours.

Twenty-five people had got themselves on the substitution list and were lined up two abreast ready to double-march out through the western gate. Somewhere twenty-five others were waiting. They would have been dragged from their beds or god-knows where at the last moment, when they believed they had escaped the call for the Transport.

The Elder nodded to Bürger. Bürger did not look at him. He merely waved his stick. The Elder led out the twenty-five reprieved men. The Elder was not a happy man. His was a very difficult task. Everyone wanted a favour. This was the ultimate favour and he spent many sleepless hours figuring out the substitutes. But by sundown all would be over and he could go again to his quarters and sleep.

Antonin didn't know it, but the twenty-five substitutes were already in the Schlojska. It was a matter of protocol that the people who had bought themselves freedom should be removed before they entered the courtyard. The door swung open and they came into the sunlight. They were mostly young. A Dane or a Dutch youth, whose hair had somehow missed cropping, stood at their head. They did not fight and bicker. They walked proudly eyeing the groups. One man, about thirty-five, with very dark hair and a wafer-thin body, had pinned a medal on his coat. It hung above the Star of David.

The Elders had picked this group carefully, under the close scrutiny of Bürger. They looked as if they could make trouble.

They stood now in a ragged set of two lines in the middle of the walkway. Two soldiers behind them and one in front.

To Antonin the group represented hope. He tried to catch the eye of the young Dane. The man was preoccupied. He too might have a plan.

Some of the children in the courtyard were beginning to cry. Antonin looked at Samuel. His face was a mask.

By now it must have been eleven o'clock.

Someone had placed a box beside Bürger. He climbed on to it and surveyed the scene.

'Silence!' he called. 'Silence.'

Antonin could hardly restrain a laugh. No one was speaking. Unless Bürger was directing his remarks against the babies who were crying! It was just the proper Nazi way to start a speech. Conditioning!

It brought Antonin's mind back to the face of the soldier in front of him. Conditioning. We are all conditioned. Conditioned to wait for the next tram to come to pick us up at the corner, conditioned to eat a meal every day, conditioned to accept any system we live in. The thoughts were racing through Antonin's brain so fast he could hardly make them register. It was as if he were in a fever. Whatever we do, wherever we live, we are conditioned. We are held captive by a system – something some of us have invented to help us live, but which has taken command of us and made us accept, with resignation or without even realising it, our limitations.

In the case of the Nazi boy in front of him, it was no different. He had been brought up to believe. And to accept. The boy was not blind. He was not specially stupid. He was accepting, just as an undertaker or a butcher accepts his lot.

Well, this is where that got you! Right here. A half-Jew, broken-down comedian staring an eighteen-year-old conditioned ripe-faced youth in the eyes. One knowing the other was about to die and the thought rolling off him like water.

Antonín could not resist it. He let the corners of his mouth sag and stuck his top teeth over his bottom lip. He crossed his eyes.

The Nazi boy's face broke into a smile.

'Number 297!'

The sergeant in charge of papers at the desk was shouting. Bürger was still on his box. Antonín hadn't heard a word he'd said. Nor had it made any impression on anyone around him from the looks on their faces.

What the hell did they want number 297 for? Antonín saw an old woman in the next group lean towards the man next to her and shout, 'That's you, dear. They're calling you.'

The old man, obviously deaf, ran at the double to the table. There was a slight argument between the sergeant and the corporal. The old man was led away.

Ten minutes went by. Antonín saw the old woman wipe her eyes with the hem of her dress. Who could tell what was going on behind all those wrinkles? And in any case perhaps she would not live to get on the Transport.

Another substitute. He was also old and he took his place awkwardly beside the old woman.

Vera whispered, 'I knew him. He was a German. She is Czech. Unless it is a political crime, even Bürger has to be careful about Germans.'

Finally orderlies came round with the numbered cards from the boxes beside the little table. Each group had been given a group of numbers.

The cards were handed round. They hung from the necks of the people like placards. Now the Germans knew each person.

But it wasn't over. Each person now had to be called to the table in the order of his number to present his papers.

'Be patient and for God's sake don't start anything,' said Vera.

'Why do they have to check again?'

'If someone is missing they will search the camp until they find him.'

'Jesus Christ!'

But Vera didn't seem to have heard. She had caught sight of one of her girls on the other side of the courtyard. She risked a wave. The girl moved her fingers slightly.

It was strange how calm it was there.

They were calling the numbers now and letting the crowds through in groups of twenty or more. People ran when their number was shouted. They stopped at the table. The old out of breath, the young in fear. They were each ordered to drop their bundle and an orderly pushed his stick into it to make sure nothing was hidden.

Of course many things were hidden. They were confiscated. A note was made beside the person's name, and he was told, 'You will get it back after the war.'

The list at the table was double-columned. On one side was a name, prepared by the Jewish Elders, with a street or block number. On the other was the number given the person and hung around his neck.

'Papers?'

The man at the table was middle-aged and very nervous. He fumbled in his pocket and produced an identity card, with a photo on it and across it, stamped in black ink, JEW.

The corporal took the papers from the man's trembling hand. The orderly poked around with his stick in the undone bundle on the cobbles.

'What's this?'

His stick pushed aside a piece of dull, heavy metal, the size of a large peanut.

'It's mine. I've had it with me for years. Sort of a charm.'

'Charm, eh?' Bürger's aide had come over. He picked it up. Taking out a knife, the orderly scraped the side of it. It shone.

The aide said, 'Where did you get this?'

There was a moment's pause.

'I worked in the mortuary.'

'Yes?'

'From the teeth.'

Bürger looked down from his box, 'You stole it from your own Jewish dead?'

'The Elders . . . they knew about it. We have been doing it for months.'

'The Elders knew?'

126

'Yes, sir . . . you can take it, Herr Kommandant . . . here, it is yours.'

Bürger's eyes met the man's. Then he turned back to the parade of wilting faces. Three thousand and sixty-seven. The largest Transport ever to leave Terezin.

The aide said, 'What shall we do with him?'

Bürger's eyes were still on the crowd. If he didn't get them on the train soon there'd be some corpses strewn around. Without turning he said, 'Oh, give him his gold. I wash my hands of it. If the Elders didn't punish him for a crime against their own race, why should I?'

The man's eyes glistened with thanks. And he shuffled back into line and then ran through the gate with the others in his group.

Antonin's group were called all together. He marched at their head refusing to let them run. He slowed slightly when passing the young Dane and said, 'I'm with you.' Then he passed on.

But before he reached the table he felt a hand come into his. . . . At first he thought it was Samuel's. Then he saw it was a boy in another group they were passing. It was so crowded in the courtyard that he hardly had time to catch the boy's face. When the hand let go, there was something in his own hand. It was his watch.

Antonin looked back over his shoulder and saw a small hand waving at him.

They were at the table. The children were processed easily. They were already numbers. Vera still had a name. So did the doctor. As their numbers were recorded, they handed over their papers which were filed in small boxes according to numbers, and made ready for transporting in a special freight car. The corporal at the desk then crossed off the name, the street and the number. In this way the person was wiped from the records at Terezin for ever. Or so the Germans thought. But in every foolproof procedure there is a grave flaw. The Jewish Elders kept a copy of their lists and, after each Transport left, buried them in a drain under the apple trees which grew on the Lagerkommandant's lawn.

'Papers?'

Antonin looked down at the head of the corporal whose forage cap failed to cover his baldness.

'I have none.'

'Papers!'

Antonin was sure now. About conditioning. He was even interested in the next question. What would the man do? The situation had not been in the manual of training. Like a salesman whose *spiel* has been interrupted by an intelligent customer, the corporal stared blankly and then, looked down.

'No papers?' he said very slowly, writing.

'Don't put that!' snapped the sergeant.

Antonin started to laugh.

'*Halt's Maul!*'

Antonin noticed that Bürger steadfastly refused to look his way.

'Sir, this man says he has no papers,' the sergeant said. Bürger said nothing.

'Sir . . . ?'

'Oh, get on with it, you fool. Put anything! . . . Put papers received and leave it at that! All these people have to be on the platform by 1400 hours.' His face almost turned to meet Antonin's stare, 'And let him keep that violin – it's an order!'

'Yes, sir.'

Antonin was still laughing.

Bürger couldn't resist it. He turned. Their eyes met.

'The word of a German officer?'

'Get him out.'

Two guards sprang forward and took Antonin under the arms.

'The word of a German officer!' Antonin screamed.

The last of his cry was heard only by those standing on the side of the road in lines, waiting to be loaded on to the wagons which stretched for nearly the length of the street.

38

Once outside the courtyard and faced with the train, it wasn't so bad. At least the formalities had been dealt with.

The street was narrow like all Terezin streets. The sunken railway lines ran down the centre, across several blocks. The other end of the line took a twist to the left and disappeared round a corner towards the gate.

Antonin found himself being led by a soldier to the rear of the train. Each wagon was covered. It had a small grill about half a metre by half a metre near the top of the door. The door of each wagon was open, revealing a straw-covered floor and a large bucket with water in it. The usual ramps leading to each open doorway had been supplemented with improvised plank-age.

People were talking out here. There were guards at each street intersection, and at each end of the train. Some were SS men, but most were Kompanie Pioniere. A few men patrolled the length of the train to make sure that no one boarded, and occasionally they herded some particularly active children off the rails.

Children were playing hop-scotch on the pavement. A couple of teenage girls were hugging and kissing each other, obviously assigned to different wagons. One man, a bull of a fellow with a neck that was as thick as his head, stood back from his belongings and glowered at people passing.

Four youths, one nonchalantly kicking at the pavement with his shoe, were talking. Another in the group was laughing. It was a relief. One pointed to a girl about thirty feet away and they all laughed.

A young mother, separated from her husband, glanced across at him smiling and then looking down coyly as if it were the first time they'd noticed each other.

Then came some more children. Younger this time, and drawing with a stick in the dirt, kneeling on their haunches and playing a game far more serious to them than the one they were actually involved in. Not far away an old woman sat on a battered suitcase. How had that come through the 'customs', wondered Antonin. How indeed had she dragged it this far? Everywhere there seemed to be movement, scurrying, and a sort of excitement.

Antonin and his group, the doctor bringing up the rear and talking constantly to the children, and Vera somewhere in the middle holding the hand of Samuel and a small girl, reached the mid point of the train, stepping over bundles and people lying on the pavement.

'Jews! Revolt! Kill them!'

The cry was loud and strong. It came from nearby. Antonin twisted his neck. A man in his forties with deep-set eyes and a prominent chin was shouting at the top of his voice.

As he ran forward towards the guard who was passing just ahead of Antonin, two others followed. They had no weapons. But the SS man was taken completely off his guard. The man hit him in the chest, knocking him back against the train. His left hand came up and he tore at the machine gun. It was anchored round the guard's neck.

The four youths had dropped their nonchalant air and started forward. The man was holding the guard against the car. People were running. Some of the old were backed off against the wall and mothers were calling to their children.

The SS guard was frightened. His eyes were bulging slightly and he was trying to shout for help. It was then that Antonin noticed that he was the same man he'd made faces at in the courtyard.

The attacker's right hand was pressed firmly under his chin, the white knuckles forcing themselves on to his wind-pipe.

Antonin shouted, 'Take the children down along the line, Vera!'

The children began to rush past him. Vera caught his arm. 'Come on. Get out of it.'

It seemed that everyone was shouting now, and Vera was pulling at his arm with a strength he hadn't suspected in her.

'Jews! Attack! Jews kill!' It had become a rhythmic chant.

As Vera pulled, Antonin saw Bürger come through the archway with two men.

He shook free of Vera's hand, but she took it again. They were now thirty feet down the line from the scuffle. The man was still throttling the guard, but the machine gun would not come off his back. Someone was trying to twist it round so that they could turn it on the SS men coming to the rescue.

Bürger shouted a command. Antonin saw the big Dane leap forward and hit the SS guard with the machine gun butt. He slid down the side of the wagon and sat forward with his head on his chest.

The Dane tore the machine gun from his hand and turned it on Bürger.

There was a burst of fire. Antonin opened his eyes to see the Dane lying dead, his blood-soaked back arched over the broken neck of the guard.

It was over in a couple of seconds. The man who had shot the Dane and saved Bürger's life was on the top of the box car above. He still stood there, with his gun poised as if he couldn't believe it.

They lined up the three other youths, the dark man with the sunken eyes and a young girl, taken at random, against the wall beside the archway. Then they stood back with their machine guns and fired at them until the firing rang in the ears of everyone there. It was still ringing minutes later, although the slumped bodies were almost empty of blood.

An orderly brought a bucket of sawdust and some straw from a wagon and spread them over the blood so that the guards wouldn't slip on it.

Bürger stood in the doorway of a wagon half way down the train. Antonin could almost touch his feet. But he was scared now. Moments ago he would have tried to topple him.

Bürger had a megaphone. 'Anyone else want to try more stupidity? I should hope you will all co-operate and act like human beings. There will be two more substitutes. Corporal, go out into the street and bring two so that we can get loaded.'

He stepped down. His foot struck Antonin on the chest as he swung off the ramp.

'Facts are facts, Karas. You will learn to accept them.' He walked up the pavement again.

Antonin recovered from his shock when he saw two children arguing over a stone which one of them had found under a wagon. He looked around him. Everything was back to normal. Children were playing. An old woman was saying a rosary. A Dutch Jew was singing to himself with his eyes shut, rocking back and forth. Women were dragging small carts with babies in them back and forth along the pavement to their proper standing place in front of the correct wagon.

'Are you all right?' said Vera.

'I'm getting there.'

'Let me dress your hand, then.'

Antonin looked down. His left hand was covered with blood.

'It's only a scratch. At first I thought the shot hit you in the chest. Your hand must have covered it.'

He looked up from his hand to her eyes.

'No one else was touched?'

'Not in our group . . .' she said.

'But in whose group?'

'Jana, the girl from my class. She was the one shot.'

The substitutes had arrived now.

'See what I mean? Just more bloodshed?'

'It will be without bloodshed. It has made me even more determined.' Antonin looked down towards the archway. An old man was coming up the line. He walked with such determination that Antonin was fascinated.

Vera had tied a rag round his hand. It was beginning to hurt.

'Here's the bullet! Want to keep it as a souvenir?' she laughed as she dug it out of the side of the wagon door with a sharp stone.

'I'll take it. It may come in handy.'

The old man was no farther away than fifteen feet. He stopped. An SS man pushed him back. He was trying to get to a group of five people standing back from the wagon and talking in low whispers.

The SS guard pushed the old man back a second time, but he came forward again as soon as the guard had passed on his patrol.

He bowed slightly before the little group. They parted and turned to listen to him. There was a lot of noise now. Antonin couldn't hear what was being said.

'We'd better get all down the line to our wagon before any more trouble breaks out . . .' said Vera.

'Wait,' said Antonin. 'What's he doing?'

'That old man?'

'Who's he bowing and scraping to? Who are they?'

'I don't know him but someone there probably saved his life or something and he wants to thank them before he leaves. Or perhaps he just wants to meet them. People do funny things at times like this!'

'Why would he want to meet them?'

'They're celebrities.'

'What sort of celebrities?'

'The man on the end, there. He's a famous surgeon from Brno. Next to him is Hemkel. . . . '

'The violinist?'

'That's him.'

'God!'

'That one behind, believe it or not, is supposed to have been a French cabinet minister . . . and let me see . . . yes the tall, proud one?'

'With the medal?'

'With the medal. He was a General. In the German army. He's a political prisoner. We have a few.'

'Hemkel?' Antonin felt Vera's hand in his again. She was pulling him towards the children, whom the doctor had taken to safety beside wagon number 48.

After that it all happened very quickly and in an orderly fashion. Women and children went into the wagons first, helped by the men. Then they were followed by old men.

Lastly the young and able.

The last person Antonin spoke to on the platform was a youth who was about to climb into the next wagon. He shouted at Antonin and at first Antonin thought another demonstration was to take place and he hurried up the ramp. But then he recognised the voice.

It was Pavel.

'Mr Karas, I heard you were here. But I couldn't find you.'

'I never knew. . . . '

'They came for me two nights after I left your apartment. I arrived here soon after you.'

'Why?'

'Those forged papers.'

'Listen. It's all round the business, Mr Karas.'

'What is?'

'About you coming here . . . as a volunteer . . . to help entertain.'

'I can't hear you!'

'Everyone thinks you're the top of the bill . . . ' shouted Pavel, and a guard pushed him inside the wagon.

Antonin stepped into the warmth of his own wagon to find that the doctor with his usual ability had already organised people into groups. Those who sat down for half an hour and those who stood up for half an hour.

Antonin stood in the doorway looking at each face in turn.

133

He smiled at Vera and touched his wounded left hand. He was proud of it and he was proud of what Pavel had said, poor bastard.

Suddenly the door slid to behind him and until their eyes grew accustomed to the darkness they all kept silent. Then some child giggled, and they all started to laugh.

The laughter lasted a long time.

Meanwhile Bürger went along the train with his aide, marking in chalk the insignia on each coach which was its coded destination.

Only Bürger knew the code. And it was merely a place on a map to him. It was called Auschwitz.

39

The train started to move without even the occupants knowing it. The Kompanie Pioniere had placed the two engines on the front on a slight decline so that all they had to do was to let off the brakes and the train would start to move of its own accord. It was outside the gates within a few minutes and the gates then closed again. All fifty wagons.

Bürger and his aide walked back to the courtyard with the Alsatian.

The pavement where the train had stood was empty save for the blood of the murdered prisoners. The body of the SS man had been taken to the morgue.

They turned into the silence of the courtyard. The snow had melted again. The table had been removed. So had the confiscated goods. At least those of any worth had been removed. The remainder lay in a shawl almost like a burial mound, near where the table had been. A man's hat was floating in the drain puddle and snow was covering it. The pigeons had come back to the courtyard. They were looking for crumbs of bread.

Bürger's foot hit something. He flipped it on its back, and bent down to pick it up. It was Antonin's watch. In his hurry Antonin had forgotten that the pocket he placed it in had a hole in it. In any case it would probably have been stolen again.

The boots of Bürger and his assistant echoed in the empty courtyard. In the distance they heard a train whistle. The Transport from Terezin had reached the main line.

And another cable lay on Bürger's desk in his office.

40

The darkness was like a blue quilt. It covered the wagon softly and brought a certain warmth as the train shuffled its way along the uneven tracks.

No one slept. The doctor tended the wound of a small girl who had cut her hand climbing into the car. The treatment was more therapeutic than medicinal.

In one corner two boys were having an argument about whose turn it was to sit down. Vera settled it. Antonin was glad. Around him the boys and girls seemed unusually passive and he was tired.

The small iron-grilled window, high up on the door, gave little air and even less moonlight. But there was enough light to see the bucket of water. Antonin's tired eyes were mesmerised by the water's sway as the train gathered speed along the few straight stretches of track.

His sole possession, his violin, was upright in its black box at his feet. His elbows rested on top of it. His chin rested in his cupped hands above his elbows. One of the children caught sight of him and began to laugh. The boy nudged his friend and the laughter began to trickle round the wagon. It brought Antonin out of his reverie.

'Sir, will you please play the violin?'

The violin? Antonin had almost forgotten he had it. He'd carried it so long that it had become part of his body.

And the thought of playing it seemed overwhelming.

'Please sir, some music?'

Antonin thought of Hemkel. Had they let him take his violin? Why would they want to take Hemkel to a camp anyway? Wouldn't they want to use his talents to keep up the spirits of the German troops and their collaborators? It was madness.

'Music! Music! Music!'

A clapping of hands in unison. His audience was waiting. There was only one answer. He'd get a few laughs while he

136

fooled around trying to tune the instrument and that would give him time to draw on what energy he could find. Where did one draw on energy? Would the mask work? He struck the C string and made it sound like a raspberry. He held the violin at arm's length and sounded it again. His face was mimicking a puzzled expression. He put his ear to the sounding box and struck again, leaping back at the rasping note.

'He's going to do jokes. Do jokes, not music!'

'No music. It's night.'

'Jokes will wake us up.'

'Do jokes, please, Mr Karas. Do jokes.'

Antonin played along for some time to let his mind settle. Jokes? After what had happened this morning and the uncertainty of their situation? Jokes? Then he remembered the face of the young German soldier. Even he had smiled. What better time for jokes?

'All right, but first some serious music, I want you all to listen carefully.' In the darkness he felt Vera stepping over the children, making her way towards him. It made him feel better knowing she was near when he was performing.

'So it is very serious! How many of you can see the violin?' he said holding it up so that the faint light from the window fell on it.

'I can.'

'So can I.'

'I can't see it. Jan, your head's in the way.'

'Jan's head's always in the way. It's the size of a sack of potatoes.'

'Then get your head tucked under your arm or something,' said Antonin.

The violin seemed to hang in the moonlit air. It's a good effect, thought Antonin, I wonder if I can get it with a spotlight in a theatre.

The violin began to play. He revolved it in the light to show that no bow was on the strings. It was Fra Diabolo's aria. It was magic.

The train lurched to the left. The violin played a wrong note. There was a roar of laughter.

'How do you do it?'

'He's got another violin.'

'No. He's playing the bow on the back.'

Antonin revolved it to show that there was no string or bow on the back.

'There's a motor. Some mechanics.'

'Well *something's* doing it.'

The music stopped. In truth Antonin had to take a breath. How many years ago was it? Did it matter? He had remembered. You twisted your tongue in your mouth and used your lips as a keyboard. It was a matter of pitch. You had to hit the same pitch as the violin and throw your voice so that it seemed to come from outside you.

They were clapping now. He started to play on the violin. A country tune, softly and with warmth. Sleepy eyes started up at him. The small girl with the cut finger was rubbing her eyes. A yawn came from in the corner where the boys had been fighting.

When the tune came to an end there was only scattered applause because Antonin had sent most of them to sleep.

'I think it's done the trick,' he said to Vera.

'It was a long day. I hope it will be a long night.'

The doctor was pulling at his elbow. 'There might be room for all of them to rest at once if we made them sit back to back. What do you think?' He was off arranging things without waiting for an answer. His quick energetic movements amazed Antonin.

Many of the children were upset at being woken, and the doctor's almost endless patience was being put to the test.

'Leave me alone!'

'For Christ's sake! Go away!' An arm was flung in his face. But the man carried on impassively, the straw brushing his knees and the water bucket being moved from place to place in the hope of making it disappear.

At last it was done. Or so it seemed. One group of boys in the centre had grabbed the place where the bucket had stood and were huddled, heads together.

'It's hard to make them understand, but they are good children. Now what are they up to?' the doctor pointed to the boys in the huddle.

'A crap game, no doubt!' said Antonin.

'Yes, something like that,' said the doctor whose intense interest in his immediate problems often obliterated his sense of humour.

'You haven't finished yet,' said Antonin.

'What? I beg your pardon, Karas?'

'What about Vera and me?'

'Oh, that *is* a problem. Well let me see. . . .'

'Oh doctor, don't worry about us, Toni was only joking.'

'Yes, of course,' the doctor gave a small laugh.

The rhythm of the train was steady now. It was impossible to see out of the high window but occasionally you could tell you were going through a tunnel or a cutting.

The forming of some plan of escape had never entirely left Antonin, although after the fiasco on the pavement at the loading ramp, he had begun to lose confidence. He looked around the wagon. The thing was solidly built. There was a small ventilation funnel in the roof, but it was not even big enough to put a hand into. The window seemed securely barred and besides he doubted if even the smallest child could be squeezed through . . . and squeezed through to what? The floor was oak, and the door presumably locked with a master key held by the Kompanie Pioniere.

If the train stopped at some place, he could shout. Maybe some resistance men would hear about the train and come and rescue them. If they went towards the eastern border of Czechoslovakia there were hundreds hiding in the woods, some of them deserters from the German army. They were an almost constant source of annoyance to the Third Reich, lighting flares to guide Allied planes to supply dumps, attacking lone patrols and occasionally making a show in some major city to keep up the spirits of the people. They had helped organise the killing of the dreaded Reichsprotektor, Heydrich, on the outskirts of Prague, an act which had brought the slaughter of the people of the village of Lidice.

'What are you thinking?' It was Vera at his side, 'I've been watching you in the darkness. Your face has been twitching like a fox sniffing the air.'

'My face never twitches.'

'It does. Whenever you start thinking.'

'It doesn't.'

'I tell you it does. Just like a fox.'

'Well, I never knew it. I was wondering which way we were going.'

'We'll know when we get there.'

There was a pause. Her hand slipped into his.

'Does it hurt you to be told you look like a fox?'

He laughed. 'It would have hurt me a few weeks ago. I'd have been very hurt. Now I'm pleased. It means someone is noticing me.' Antonin changed the subject quickly. 'Is that

Samuel there in the centre planning the great something-or-other?'

'Yes, and Heinrich and Jan.'

'If I lift him up to the window maybe we can see where we are.' Antonin leant over and tapped Samuel on the corner. The boy's blue eyes flicked round to him tensely.

'Samuel, I want you to help me.'

'I want you to help me too.' Samuel stood up. 'You see that window, I want to look through it. Heinrich has been counting the number of tracks we've passed. He's not a very accurate counter, but he's an expert on trains. His father was an engineer and there isn't much he doesn't know. He says each length of track is usually fifteen metres. We've been over four thousand. That means we've gone about sixty kilometres . . . if we've been averaging fifty kilometres an hour. . . .'

The child's ingenuity amazed Antonin.

'So, please sir, lift me up to the window?'

Antonin leant towards him and helped him over the sleeping children.

'We are going downhill, I heard them turn down the steam pressure. See if you can see any lights,' said Heinrich.

Antonin stood under the window and hoisted Samuel to the grill. He clung on to it with his fists and put his nose through.

'It's sure cold.'

There was a pause.

'Can't see a thing.'

'To your right . . . look down below. To the right.'

Antonin's arms were shaking with the exertion.

'Keep steady, Mr Karas . . . now . . . now I can see . . . yes lights. A few lights . . . a river. A big river. Just up ahead.'

'OK. That's good, now come down.'

Antonin lowered the boy to the floor.

'Lights? Prague?' said Vera.

But the boys didn't answer. Samuel had hopped back excitedly to the group in the middle of the wagon.

'Once we've crossed that bridge . . . you'll hear it by the sound of the wheels . . . we'll be on the eastern bank of the Moldau . . . that means Prague,' said Heinrich.

'Are you Czech?' asked Vera.

'No,' said Heinrich, 'but I used to follow my father's trips on maps he had. He told me everything about every place he went. Where he stopped the night, where he took on fuel and all about the sidings and things like that.'

140

'And you remember it all?'

'Most things.' The boy was undoing his shirt. 'Now, if we are approaching the eastern bank there is a siding about two miles up the line where we'll take on coal. . . . '

Antonin was fascinated. His head was down at the level of the straw looking up at Heinrich. Heinrich was feeling under his armpit.

He produced a compass.

He placed it on the floor, clearing aside the straw to make a level spot.

'How long have you had that?' said Antonin.

'I've kept it under my arm ever since we left home.'

Antonin felt he was interrupting something important and that he should keep his mouth shut. The concentration on the boys' faces was complete.

'When we leave the siding, we'll have to listen carefully. If the train turns left we're on our way to Germany. If it turns to the right the line takes us through Czechoslovakia to the Polish border. That means Poland.' Heinrich put his compass back under his armpit and buttoned his shirt. 'My guess is that we're off to Poland. We'll be reaching the bridge any minute. These engines are 456's and they are capable of speeds up to eighty kilometres, but with this load we'll probably average about fifty.'

Heinrich brushed the dust from the straw off his hands and sat down. 'Better do what the doctor ordered,' he said glancing over his shoulder at the standing doctor who was snoring peacefully asleep.

The other children sat down.

'You are very clever boys,' said Antonin. 'My congratulations.'

'Sir?'

'Yes, Heinrich?'

The tone of the question was a boy's again. Previously — while serious matters were at hand – it had been adult.

'Sir, is it hard to get on the stage?'

'You should hear him sing,' said Samuel. 'He's got a voice like an angel.'

'Angel, my arse,' said Jan. 'It's like a fog horn.'

'It's pretty strong, anyway.'

'Then you can sing like an angel in a fog,' said Antonin, 'yes, and it's hard to get on the stage, but if you want anything enough, you'll make it.'

They heard the first clang of the wheel as the train passed over the bridge.

'Jesus! You're right,' said Jan.

'Say, let's count the rails until we reach the siding; see if Heinrich is right.'

Antonin rose to his feet and in one leap made the door. Prague! They would be passing through Prague. He knew the line.

I must see! I've got to see Prague, he said to himself. He began to claw his way up the wooden door towards the window. His nails gave way and he slipped. He tried again almost in desperation. His left hand nails caught in the grain. The splinters dug into the flesh. He grabbed with his right. His shoe kept slipping and he was hanging for a fraction of a second with his left hand. He hardly felt the pain. The excitement and the panic was all he could sense. He jumped up again, hoping to catch his right hand in the grill, but fell hopelessly and knocked over two sleeping children who began to cry.

The doctor woke suddenly. 'What in hell's name . . . ?'

'I've got to see it. See it . . . Prague!'

'You idiot, you're causing a panic. Get away from the window.' It was Vera.

But Antonin made one more leap. His right hand caught a nail and it went into the flesh of his little finger. He turned in desperation.

Vera said, 'Why don't you let me lift you. The doctor will help.'

'Eh? What's that?' The pain of Antonin's bruises was coming to him now. His injured left hand was covered with blood again and the splinters were deep under his nails.

'No. No. I'm sorry. I'll lift you. You want to see too. After all it's a long time. No, I insist. I'll lift you.'

The doctor was calming the startled children.

Vera came and stood in front of him, facing the door and looking up at the small window.

Antonin tensed his toes against the door. He caught Vera round the waist but her skirt slipped up. He tried again lower down her body, beneath the knees. She managed to claw the window bars.

She stayed like that for a few seconds. Antonin had his arms clasped round her legs and his face rested on one side of her right thigh.

'What can you see?' he whispered hoarsely.

'The river. It's grey. The castle is blacked out and so are most of the streets. There's a light ahead . . . it's the end of the bridge.'

'Can you really see the city itself?' It was the doctor trying to take some of the load off Antonin. Antonin brushed him aside.

'I can now, like a long-necked monster with horns all down its back.'

'But the people? Are there no people around?' said the doctor.

'Not a soul.'

'There's a curfew,' said Antonin.

'You two have a look now,' said Vera coming down. She slid gently down Antonin's body and her feet touched the floor and remained beside Antonin's for a split second.

The doctor said, 'I'd rather not. Thank you though.'

'Why not?' asked Vera.

'Just that . . . I'm not Czech!'

'How about you, Toni?'

'No. Now that you've seen it. . . . '

'Listen . . . !' It was Heinrich almost shouting his whisper.

The train was drawing to a stop. They were in the siding.

'And in any case what is there to see here? One railway yard is like another.'

'I quite agree,' said the doctor.

Antonin was annoyed with the doctor for some reason. Even this mundane remark annoyed him. Why had he tried to help him hold Vera up against the door? Didn't the fool think he could manage alone?

Vera was examining his fingers now and trying to stop the flow of blood so that she could pull out the splinters. She had concealed a bone needle under the hem of her skirt and it wasn't very sharp.

Antonin tried to make as little noise as possible, but he was always frightened by pain.

Half an hour later they started to pull out of the siding. The train backed its own length down the line, and then slowly started forward.

Most of the children were still asleep. But Samuel and his friends were standing up. As the train pulled forward again it began to turn right. It was a sharp curve and everyone could feel it and hear the wheels grinding on the rails.

Samuel said quietly, 'Poland!'

143

Hurriedly Antonin said, 'You are going home.'

'To Poland, but not to home.'

Heinrich was licking his lips . . . Jan flicked a piece of straw off his nose. Then Samuel spoke again.

'To Poland, and to gas.'

Antonin watched Samuel's face, knowing there was nothing he could do to help. He was still watching when Samuel finally sat down and he and Heinrich snuggled together to sleep. Antonin backed against the door. His hands were swollen and he was exhausted. He looked around the sleeping wagon. The children were like a lot of mice in a burrow, caught up together and tangled in a web of sleep.

All he could think about was the smell of Vera's hair as her head had passed his on its way up to look out of the window.

41

It was sunny. Almost spring-like, but cold. Bürger stood in the doorway of his headquarters. He was dressed in a Lovatt-green Harris tweed hunting jacket, knickerbocker trousers, green tartan stockings, set off with pheasant's feathers at the garter, and a knitted tie. His Meerschaum pipe was filled and in his mouth. But it had gone out: a detail he was not going to let put him off.

The orderly on the gate had phoned to say that there were seven cars coming. One would be for Herr Eichmann and his aide. There would be one used as an escort in the rear. The other five cars could contain as many as twenty people. Bürger was worried. And it was colder than he thought. He had no civilian overcoat and he did not want to spoil the effect by donning a military greatcoat.

He could actually hear the cars coming now. Everything had been rehearsed. To the last detail. Nothing could go wrong. At 1305 hours the first car appeared round the corner. It was the escort car from the gate and Bürger nodded to it, throwing a grandfatherly wave to his aide in the front seat.

The second car contained Herr Eichmann. It was, of course, a large enclosed Mercedes, the flag of the Third Reich on a thin silver pole on the radiator cap. The bullet proof windows did not reflect the sun.

Herr Eichmann was taller than he had suspected. He was a typical bureaucrat or banker. Silver-rimmed glasses, greying hair, thin lips and a compromising nose.

As he stepped out, the chauffeur holding the door, Bürger noticed the cape. Also Harris tweed, but of Scottish not German cut, the sort most English countrymen were depicted wearing with deerstalker hats.

Bürger had an automatic reflex which almost caused him embarrassment. He began to salute. But with his hand half-way to his shoulder he stiffly held it out.

Eichmann's handshake was limp. The other cars had drawn up in the square now and a small fussy man was coming towards him. It was Georges Sussens.

Sussens was business-like and crisp. He had with him two aides, three members of the Swedish Red Cross, a Portuguese and four women whose nationality Bürger never discovered. The visit was a precedent. It had been two years since Bürger had entertained so many dignitaries, so he left the introductions to his daughter, who stood behind him in Czech national costume with wild daisies in a garland round her flaxen hair.

The Jewish Elders of the town were introduced in the hallway. Dr Hertzog shook hands with Sussens and exchanged a few words about the weather. The remainder were silent.

They proceeded immediately to a luncheon of roast mutton, potatoes and cabbage, all of which Bürger proudly proclaimed to be local produce.

'If there's one thing we are able to produce above all other here at Terezin, it's good fresh vegetables. Is that not so, Dr Hertzog?'

The doctor nodded, knowing as he did that the mutton had come originally from Lidice, and that in truth there was a Jewish girl tending the sheep in the field outside the walls behind Bürger's house.

A wine was offered with the meal. It was delicious, a Moravian grape, noted for its crisp dryness and rounded *gout*. But it was declined by most, the Pilsener beer being preferred, as it was very hard to get, and as Pilsen was only thirty-two kilometres from Terezin.

At 1400 hours, the meal having been cleared away, the programme for the afternoon was outlined by Bürger's aide. It was safer this way. Should anything happen to go wrong, it left Bürger a loophole.

At 1430 hours, after some discussion about the route, which seemed complex in places, the party set out on foot.

In the hallway, as another touch of informality, Bürger's secretary handed him a flat box. It contained candy.

Outside, the sun was still shining and the film crew which had come from the Propaganda Ministerium was ready to shoot the important International Red Cross dignitaries starting their inspection of the camp.

The shops had been opened all round the square, and on cue those destined to act as people enjoying the vacation proclaimed in honour of the Red Cross visit were parading about.

A young couple, dressed in overcoats and good strong boots, walked with their arms around each other down the main street, chatting and laughing. A woman with a shopping bag went into the baker's shop and soon (a bit too soon according to Bürger's recollection) came out with a loaf of newly-baked white bread.

On the snow-covered grass in the centre of the square sat an old man. He had been given some bread crumbs to feed the pigeons. But he had been hungry and had eaten them all.

There was a small Baroque church at the east end of the square. Its doors had been opened and the cleaning people had done an excellent job of making the steps look used.

Bürger began to relax and to join in the theatricals. He waved to two young people standing on the church steps discussing a magazine. They waved back.

He grinned. No one would have recognised his clerk Hans Alsen or Corporal Josef Weber any more than they were recognising other German soldiers mingled in with the rest of the actors.

A group of musicians was taking the stand and turning up for the concert. Every instrument had arrived from Prague in good shape, with the exception of one trombone which was stuffed with cement. Bürger had positioned the player in the rear and was sure that no one would notice.

As they left the main square of the camp, the Swiss Sussens stopped a middle-aged couple on the street and asked them how they were enjoying their lives.

'We are enjoying ourselves. Thank you so much for the vacation.'

With a quick glance over his shoulder at the green wooden wall which cut off the rest of the camp, Bürger led the party into the school. It was indeed the real school. But desks had been found and pictures were hanging on the walls. Bürger's daughter went down the rows of standing children and ran her hand over the shaven heads of the boys, stopping to turn the pages of a copy book. Seeing it was blank, she flipped it back to the original page.

The children sang a traditional Czech song for the visitors. It was a tune which Sudeten Germans knew, and the children were applauded and duly thanked by Sussens.

Out into the good fresh air of the Czech countryside again as the party made its way to the bank. Here, the Swiss delegation paused.

'You would like to enter? Please?' Bürger gave a bow.

Inside, the party met Karel Bobicek, the manager, and they examined the notes which had been printed in Prague. The words THERESIENSTADT were printed inside an empty oval in the middle of the notes.

Sussens held the notes up to the light. They were genuine. 'Don't suppose they are worth much on the international market yet?'

'No sir.'

'Well, one day, who knows? Thank you.'

The Swiss party passed out into the street again where a group of very small children were playing hop-scotch. Bürger handed round some candies which the children accepted with little curtsies.

Once again, with his eyes on the green wall, Bürger led the party to the benches which had been prepared in the main square so that the International Red Cross visitors should be allowed to hear part of a concert that had been prepared by the inhabitants of Theresienstadt for the vacation.

It was a most impressive rendering of a suite by Debussy, and Bürger was especially pleased, as were his guests, by the talent of a young 'guest' conductor from the Prague Symphony, one of the camp cooks.

By this time the people walking the square were beginning to appear for the second time and Bürger quickly called a halt.

'It is not on the programme but I know my daughter Inge has prepared it as a surprise,' he added. 'A cup of real English tea.'

'English tea?' asked a Swede. 'How did you come by that?'

The young Swede had been eyeing her ever since the party had started its walk.

'If you promise not to tell daddy, I'll let you into the secret,' she said.

'Word of honour,' said the Swede.

'It's out of a Red Cross parcel. A young man here who does some work in our garden got it, and he insists on giving me things from his parcels . . . daddy gets very mad.'

'Is he handsome?'

'Who?'

'The gardener.'

They were entering the safe confines of headquarters again. Bürger was in top form.

'You must all be tired, but the people have so looked forward to this visit. After tea we are to see the start of a soccer match

148

between the Jewish champion team and our soldiers. There's great rivalry. . . . '

'We'd very much like to see a dormitory and the hospital,' put in one woman.

'Yes, and the evening meal being served . . . ' put in another.

'Can't deviate from the programme too much,' said Sussens, 'but if this is at all possible. . . . '

What diplomats you Swiss people are, thought Bürger.

'Certainly, it has already been arranged. The place is yours for the day. Now, my dear, the tea?'

Inge was being the perfect *Hausfrau*. She never heard her father's next remark.

'My daughter is really amazing. Imagine, gentlemen, she gets this tea imported from Turkey, from our embassy – where she has a friend – does she not? . . . ' he wagged his finger. 'Imagine what the English tea merchant who sold it to the Turkish importer would think if he saw us now!'

Bürger roared with laughter. He was joined rather heartily by one of the Swedish delegation.

After tea, Eichmann tossed a coin for the kick-off in the soccer match, noting with thanks that there were enough soldiers on both sides to stop anything serious occurring. The women were taken to a bath house, the hospital and the dining room, which had been converted from the soldiers' kitchen.

The party left the gates of Terezin at 1800 hours. They were exhausted by the ordeal and the journey to Prague was accomplished in a little less than one hour. Here after a short rest they were entertained at a banquet.

Not one of them ever once asked to see what was behind that straight, long, wooden green wall, not even Herr Eichmann.

42

Antonin opened his eyes to feel the sunlight reflected against the snow as it bounced through the window of the wagon.

How long had he slept? One hour? Two? His watch would have been a useful asset to the group.

'Any idea where we are, Heinrich?'

Heinrich sat with his arms around his knees. Many of the children were standing now and chewing on their remnants of bread.

The doctor had piled straw near the door and it had been used as a urinal. He was organising again. Girls to the left . . . boys to the right. The children were paying very little attention, and most of them let fly where they were standing.

Heinrich turned slowly to Antonin, 'Very soon we will be at Ostrava. It is then only a matter of kilometres to the Polish border.'

'You have a plan?'

'He won't tell us. Ask him, Mr Karas,' said Samuel.

'He'll tell us when he's got it all figured out.'

'I wouldn't tell my own mother!'

'Well, I wouldn't either.'

Quickly, Heinrich turned on him, 'You got a plan, Mr Karas?'

'Not exactly. I'm thinking.'

'You'd better let me know.'

'I will. You're a good boy, Heinrich. I like you.'

'Yeah, so I know the ropes about trains!'

'Do you think someone would like you just for that?'

'Did anyone pay any attention to me before? I got it all figured out. That's life to me. Ever hear the name Heinrich before? It's German. Right? It's not my real name. I don't want no goddamn Polish name. I want a German name. It's safe and then I can be someone.'

'You are someone whatever your name is,' said Antonin.

'And so who are you to know? Did you volunteer to come here? From your safe stage job? No. They made you.'

'I didn't want to, but I'm glad I did, Heinrich.'

'More fool you. You could be having fun out there on that stage . . . with all them lights and things and women screaming out at you laughing their sides in. . . . '

'I'm still glad I did.'

Heinrich looked at him again and spat out a piece of straw, 'You're a goddamn fool, Mr Karas. . . . '

'You just shut up, Heinrich! . . . ' said Samuel.

Heinrich held up his hand and grinned, 'I'd have done the same thing . . . the same foolish thing!'

Vera woke up with a start. The train had suddenly picked up speed.

'Is there any water, my throat's parched.'

'Someone kicked the bucket over in the night, there's none left.'

Antonin thought about what Heinrich had said for a long time that day, and he also wondered what he would eventually give the boy as an answer.

By evening the train came to a dead halt in a pine forest. The wind was blowing so hard it was rocking the wagons. And with it came snow. Heavy snow. It blew in the window and every child was lifted up by the doctor or Antonin to get a mouthful. It saved the lives of two children.

Their lips were swollen so much they could hardly pry them open to let the snow fly in. The doctor was afraid it might be typhoid.

It was the coldest night Antonin had ever spent. Every time he tried to get warmth from Vera, it seemed she'd fallen asleep with her head in his hands.

43

Bürger looked up from his desk. He had written on his blotting paper, in his boldest handwriting, something that he must burn.

He had written, 'Ten thousand before the end of January. Another ten thousand before the end of February.'

He tore that section of blotting paper away and burned it.

The aide merely said, 'Ten thousand?' and coughed discreetly. 'That's not going to be easy.'

'The project being built here, on the other side of the wall, has been stopped. It is too dangerous. It must all be done at Auschwitz. I've been told this from Berlin.'

'I'm sure we can arrange the Transports somehow, sir.'

'This place will be under surveillance for months.' He paused, 'Ever think about it, Hans?'

'In what way do you mean, sir?'

'Does it ever hit you . . . I mean they *are* people.'

'Does it you, sir?'

'I suppose it's quite right. Look how they ruined the bloody country . . . and still are ruining things. Even the Elders here . . . no, it's just that at night . . . I sometimes get dreams and Inge wakes me . . . and then of course it's all right again. I suppose there's a weakness in us all. Shakespeare, wasn't it? They tell me the Russians say they invented Shakespeare or something of the sort. Now there's something goddamn stupid!'

Bürger went to the window in characteristic pose.

The aide said, 'You know, sir, the visit the other day was an unqualified success. I mean we really put on a show!' The aide was laughing.

Bürger said quietly, 'I know. That's what started the dreams. Who in hell do we think we're damn well deceiving?'

44

They had been going uphill all morning. The train was taking the climb at a steady pace, throwing up the snow on the banks of pines, and spewing out soot from its engines. The second locomotive had been put behind, pushing the train along the gradient.

Around noon they passed through Jesenik. The Polish border lay some thirty kilometres to the north, but they had to wind their way up through the Tatra mountains to get to it. The first large town on the other side would be the industrial centre of Cracow.

Conditions in the wagon had deteriorated. There had been more vomiting and in spite of the doctor's strict orders about the rationing of the last pieces of bread, the children had gulped down what they had left.

The straw in the bottom of the wagon had been turned twice, and was now so sodden that it was moulding.

Antonin had struggled for a plan. But they were trapped. The only chance they had was if the train stopped and they came to open the doors to change the straw. They would have to do it sooner or later. They would also have to bring some bread. He wondered how many of the children were well enough to make a rush for it. Five, including two girls, could hardly stand.

The one piece of luck they had was that it didn't appear to be typhoid. Temperatures were fairly normal and diarrhoea was not acute. It was simply exhaustion.

'There comes a point,' said the doctor, 'when the will says "I give up" and the body obeys and lies in decay.'

This was not the first such railway journey the children had taken, of course, and this helped the strong ones.

'Still going to try to get us out of here?' Vera had no trace of sarcasm in her voice.

'There's a way. It will come. I'm sure of it,' but Antonin spoke with an empty heart. The mask was wearing thin.

The train came to a halt suddenly. Heinrich jumped to his feet. It rolled back on the hill a few metres, and then the Kompanie Pioniere applied the air brakes. The train held on the ice-covered rails.

'What's happening?'

'Have we got there?'

'Maybe they ran out of coal?'

'*Shush!*' Antonin held his finger to his lips, 'please listen.'

Steam pressure on both engines was being reduced quickly. You could hear the hissing brown liquid from the boiler crackling among the tree branches.

But Antonin could hear something else. Aircraft.

'Listen!' he shouted.

There was a pause.

'Let's hope they're the Allies,' said Vera.

'What does it matter? All bombs are the same,' said Samuel.

'There's a hell of a lot of them . . . ' the doctor began.

The first bomb hit the line ahead of the train. In wagon 48 they could hear the mud and snow being blown on to the tops of the other wagons.

All the children were on their feet, some clutching others round the waist for support. Many of them started to cry.

'Quiet! Quiet! Crying won't help!' shouted the doctor.

But they cried all the more.

The first bomb was followed by a dozen or so more. The wagons lurched crazily to one side like a chain being twisted. There was suddenly a great deal of shouting outside the wagon and soldiers were running up and down.

Antonin shouted, 'Everyone stand still and listen to me. Do exactly as I say.'

From the way the wagon tilted and the screaming that was coming from up ahead it was obvious that at least one wagon had been hit and was probably on its side.

Antonin stuck his ear to the door. He could hear bolts being pulled back.

'All outside! All outside! *Lauf! Lauf!*'

More bombs fell. There was a deafening explosion ahead. Wagon 48 began to roll backwards down the hill with the three other wagons behind it and the engine that had been pushing them.

Antonin could still hear the soldier banging at the bolt. 'It's an air raid,' he kept repeating.

The wagon came to a stop. The engineers must have found

enough leverage to brake on the slippery rails.

'Listen children. Do what I say. Obey no one else. This is our chance,' said Antonin. He turned to Vera. 'I told you it'd come.'

The door of the wagon swung open revealing a stand of pines not twenty metres away. They sloped gently up a hill, their boughs heavy with crystal-white snow.

Antonin felt a machine gun in his belly. The soldier who had opened the door was standing in the doorway.

He stepped back.

'Everyone get out. *Schnell!*' said the soldier.

Antonin said, 'Com'n follow me.' He jumped down into the snow. The children began to follow. The doctor and Vera were handing those unable to make the leap into his arms. 'Run into the trees,' Antonin kept repeating.

He looked ahead at the rest of the train. Two wagons were on their sides and the front engine was in the ditch, billowing steam. A few soldiers stood at a safe distance throwing snow on live coals which had been blown on to one of the collapsed wagons.

From wagon 48 to the end, where the second engine still held bravely to tracks, they were completely cut off from the rest of the train. The tracks had been torn up and now formed a small roller-coaster in between. Just ahead of them, half hidden by the pines, was a small station.

'That's Glucholazy,' said Heinrich. 'It used to be the last station before the border. It was a customs point . . . my father. . . .'

Antonin did not listen to the rest of it. He was too busy carrying children to the pines.

Everywhere he looked there were men with machine guns. There must have been at least a dozen in the trees, and others ran up and down the train shouting.

The panic up ahead had not yet subsided. Where the two wagons had been overturned, they were dragging out the dead and injured, and putting them on the snow near the small platform.

The smell of smoke, burning rubber and hot metal filled Antonin's nostrils.

There was a shout up ahead and a terrible scream. The engine exploded and fire began to creep down the wagons. Three young prisoners grabbed a machine gun. They were firing wildly as they ran up the hill behind the station to the cover of the trees.

They never made it. The gun jammed as the last man turned to fire, and they were shot down from the tops of the wagons.

Antonin lifted down the last child and made a dash for the trees. He was followed by the doctor and the soldier who had been standing by his side.

The violin!

He began to run back to the wagon but was stopped by the German.

'My violin. I've left my violin!'

He was tapped on the elbow. It was Samuel. He was holding the violin case.

'You gave it to me. Just as I jumped down.'

Antonin was about to take it from the boy, but something in the boy's eyes stopped him.

'You keep it for me,' he said. 'Never give it to anyone else!'

Samuel's face lit up. 'I'll look after it for you. I promise.'

The planes came back again as they all stood under the trees. But it was only to look at the damage. They were B 29's from an American squadron and had been on their way to bomb Cracow.

It was a good job they had disposed of all their bombs, because people were still crawling from the wreckage and others lay trapped under twisted steel. The majority of those who could walk were herded into the station compound. Small fires were lit and a ration of bread handed round. Some of it even reached the isolated group of children in the trees.

The old and the lame climbed back into the warmth of the wagons wherever they could. They lay on the stinking straw and cursed the Allies and the Germans and even the God who had made them. Many of them died like that and their frozen bodies were dragged out later on to be put beside the tracks. Others snuggled into each other and survived.

Behind the stand of pines was a small barn of the sort used to collect hay in the summer. It had no loft, just a dried earth floor and a huge beam running the length of it with a pulley on it for the bales of hay.

The children were herded into single file and marched at the double to the barn. The sick were carried by the stronger ones, and Samuel was the envy of the group because he carried Antonin's violin.

'Why don't they shoot us all and get rid of their problem now?'

The doctor laughed.

'You don't yet understand the German mentality,' said Vera. They had nearly reached the barn. 'Once you've got X number of prisoners to account for, you have to deliver X number, not Y or Z.'

'But even if they are all going to the gas. . . . '

'Especially if they are going to their death. An escapee – just one man – can give away the secret. Why do you think they've been so careful to isolate us?'

They were inside the barn now. It was bigger than the wagon, and spotlessly clean.

There were no windows. The door was slammed behind them and a sentry placed there. But through the cracks in the logs, where the moss chinking had fallen away, they could see a meadow stretching up ahead of them, and then some more trees. The snow had blown off the meadow and tufts of dried grass stood in mounds – a frozen filigree against the skyline.

'They have cows in this meadow in summer,' said Samuel.

'How do you know?' said Vera.

'Those mounds of thick grass. They grow out of their manure. My grandfather told me that.'

'Where's the doctor?' said Antonin quickly.

'Outside,' said Vera, 'with Anna. There was no sense in letting everyone know. She was dead in the wagon. But he wanted to make sure. There are some rocks in the corner of the meadow, behind the tree. He's covering her with them. He'll be finished in a moment.'

Antonin was becoming used to it now. He didn't let the thought stick inside his head. He passed over it, as if it were something he had read in a book, or seen on a film. It had no relationship to reality. One had to acknowledge it and pass on to the next thing. The trouble was that there wasn't always a next thing to do. Unless you counted waiting. So instead Antonin took over the doctor's role and began to organise the children into groups, busying about with Vera at his side, like a mother hen. This was no routine; no comic sketch dragged from the past. It was reality. Not very exciting reality, but important nevertheless.

By the time the doctor had reappeared, Vera had big girls separated from boys, and small boys and girls all in one group. And they were chewing on the bread given to them in the trees.

157

Vera also arranged it so that her group, who spread their hay and lay on it under Vera's supervision, was next to the group under Antonin's supervision. In this way Antonin and Vera ended up sitting down side by side that afternoon and resting quietly in the warm smell of the hay.

45

It had stopped snowing. And the wind dropped. Vera heard the sentry come to relieve his comrade. He told him it was supper time, so she figured it must be around seven.

For a long time Antonin had lain beside her on the hay and stared at the beam which ran the length of the barn, his face twitching in thought.

She couldn't see the doctor because he was over on the other side of a pile of hay at the end of the barn. But she could hear him. He was snoring heavily as usual. The poor man was exhausted. He had come to her with some of Anna's clothing, which he had secreted in his pockets. 'In a day or two, when the children have forgotten, you can make use of these. Specially the socks. There's a girl here. . . . '

'Yes, also called Anna,' interrupted Vera. 'She needs some.'

Then the doctor had crawled back in the hay, careful not to wake any of the children, and fallen asleep.

Vera raised herself quietly on one elbow. She could see Samuel, the outline of his face almost angelic, on the other side of Antonin. He jumped slightly in his sleep, but his breathing was even.

'They're all asleep,' she whispered.

'What?' said Antonin.

She put her hand in his, 'They're asleep. All of them.'

The warmth of Antonin's hand was good. She had lain there for a long time unable to think of anything else but touching him. But she had not dared break his silence. The desire to touch him was too great though. And the more she tried to push it away the more she found she could not control it. It surged up along the inside of her thighs and up inside her stomach. It caressed her breasts gently so that the tips stood up taut and hard. And when it came to her head and she analysed it, she realised that what she wanted was to be touched by him. To feel him touching *her*.

159

'They're asleep, Antonin,' she repeated and as he turned his face to her she kissed him on the lips. It was a soft kiss, but Antonin could feel the energy pent up behind it. Their lips parted slowly and almost immediately she came back for more, this time sucking at his mouth, drawing the breath out of him.

'Someone'll hear.'

'No they won't. And if they do it won't be the first time,' she said.

He had rolled over in the hay now and his hand was undoing her blouse. His right leg came over hers, inside her thigh, up high. She liked the feeling of the hard knee there.

His hand was touching the tips of her breasts, the way she'd imagined, only it was better. He spread his fingers and drew the breasts together, so that one hand caressed both nipples at the same time. Her mouth was open, but she had to bite against the hay to hold on.

He put his head on her breasts and rubbed his ear over them. Then he kissed them. She was tingling. In no particular place. All over. There was only one part to her.

'We shouldn't, really, we shouldn't!' But he didn't mean it now. They'd gone too far.

His tongue was rough and hard on her nipples. He was fumbling at another button on her blouse. She drew her hands down her body and undid it for him. She loosened the top button on her skirt.

He was travelling slowly down her body now. His hands on her hips, smoothing the flesh.

She let her arms fall to her sides for a second.

'Please God make it go on. Please God!'

Her hand was on his penis. She hugged it to her bare stomach. It was so hard and thick. She must hold on.

'Dear God, life is beautiful. It's all beauty.'

Antonin's knees were gently forcing her legs apart. The penis was hot against her thigh.

It entered her body slowly and her body opened to receive it.

She could hold on no longer. . . . It had been in her mind for such a time, lying there. She felt herself pulsing inside, and then Antonin pulsing too. One, two, three, four . . . she lost count and lay back, one hand in her mouth, biting to stop herself screaming with joy.

When it was all over, Antonin rolled back on the hay and lay on his back.

'I love you, Vera,' he said.

She came back on her right elbow and smiled down at him.

'How is it that your teeth are sparkling white when you've never had anything to clean them with for years?'

'I'm just lucky I guess.'

'Did you hear what I said just now? I love you.'

'I know. And I'm so happy, Toni.'

She lay back again on the hay. Side by side they remained silent for a few minutes.

Antonin's eyes were on the beam again. Some plan was beginning to work itself out in his head.

Vera looked across at him again and to her shock saw that Samuel was sitting up.

'I couldn't sleep.'

Antonin jumped round.

'You little! . . . How long have you? . . . '

'Leave him alone!' Vera was straightening her skirt.

Antonin sat with his face near Samuel's. They stared at each other for a second. Then Antonin looked down. It was he who was embarrassed.

'You should try to sleep,' said Vera.

'I can't. It upset me. About Anna, I mean.'

Antonin smiled at him and ruffled his head. 'Then come and talk to us a bit.'

The boy slithered down the hay to their feet. Vera drew close and took his hand.

Samuel said, 'I remember . . . my mother and father . . . only . . . at that time I didn't really understand. . . . '

'You will one day, Samuel,' said Antonin.

'Oh, I do now.'

There was a short silence between them as they remained with their own thoughts, all three content to be there and not wanting to trespass on the other.

Samuel then said, 'If you have a baby, what will happen to it?'

Antonin laughed. He scratched his head.

Vera said quickly, 'I shall call him Samuel.'

All three laughed now.

'Hey, where's my violin?'

'Here!' Samuel held up his left hand which clutched the case handle. 'You don't think I'll let that go, do you?'

Samuel yawned suddenly.

'Com'n, lie down here between us.' Samuel crawled up

between them with his violin case. He lay down immediately.

When Vera looked over at Antonin to see if he was still studying the beam, he was asleep. So was Samuel. She was complete.

46

At dawn, most walking prisoners were put to work repairing the track ahead of the train. Others dug a pit into which the frozen bodies of the dead were slung.

The train Kommandant, a Lieutenant from the Kompanie Pioniere, had been in field-telephone contact with Bürger. Also with his own Kommandant in Prague. The train was to proceed as quickly as a new engine could be shunted from Cracow. There followed a list of other minor instructions which the Lieutenant did not bother his head with now. First things first. The prisoners must be made to re-lay the track ready for the engine from Cracow.

Every shovel and pick in the village must be commandeered. Every working man in the village must be put to work. The piece of humped track ahead of wagon 48 which severed the last part of the train was the toughest task. It would require completely new track. They had promised to send it with the shunted engine from Cracow.

By midday there were fifty-three shovels at work, each man taking an hour and then breaking while his partner took over. Also there were twelve picks. The village of Glucholazy was amazingly empty when the party of soldiers visited it to look for volunteers. They eventually found six men.

It was the first time that some of the prisoners had held picks in their hands for years. Shovels like these too were almost a novelty for some.

The instruments were being handled in front of the Kompanie Pioniere soldiers with a good amount of care and thought. After all the only SS man on the train was the documentation officer, and the prisoners could see that the Engineers hadn't the experience or the cunning of the SS.

47

Antonin stood on the pile of hay and jumped up, swinging like
a monkey on the beam. The children were so used to his tricks
by now that they sniggered and went on playing a guessing
game which one of them had invented.

Antonin bent his knees back and jerked his body up on to the
beam. There was nearly a metre between his body and the roof.
At the other end the beam disappeared through a small door.
The hay was lifted in bales off a cart and pushed along the beam
on the pulley, finally landing wherever the farmer wanted it in
the barn. Just how far the beam stuck out, outside the barn,
Antonin couldn't remember.

As he crawled along the children began to watch and become
silent. He motioned with his hand for them to keep talking.

At the door, he paused and put his ear to it. In spite of the
continued talking he could feel the eyes of the children on him.
There was someone coughing not too far from the little door.
He pushed gently. To his surprise it swung open silently.

Below, not two metres away was a soldier with a machine
gun. The soldier coughed again and spat on the snow.

To his left, Antonin could see the train and the prisoners
working on the tracks. According to his reckoning from what
he'd learned of German army routine, this soldier would not
change guard duty for another hour, and all other soldiers
seemed preoccupied with the work on the train. It was all
perfect.

Antonin did not shut the door again. He signalled to keep
the chatter going. He swung down to where Vera and the
doctor were waiting.

'You're a fool. You might have been killed there.'

'Listen, Vera, are you with me?'

'What do you mean?'

'It's not worth playing any tricks, Toni,' said the doctor. It
was the first time that he had used the abbreviation. 'This is not

the theatre. Those people mean business.'

'I've a plan. And now's the time. The perfect time. It may be our only chance.'

'Please, Toni, you'll get yourself killed!'

Antonin looked at her, remembering the softness of her body and the love he felt. 'I know. But if I don't we'll all be killed.'

'It isn't for sure.'

'Don't be stupid, of course it's for sure. They're going to get rid of the lot of us. What are they going to do? Keep on isolating us . . . until they win the bloody war or lose it?' He paused and blew into his fingers. 'We're wasting precious time.'

Vera said, 'Very well, I'm with you. What's the plan?'

'The plan? First, I've something to do and then I'll tell you,' said Antonin.

Antonin was up on the beam again before the doctor could stop him. The doctor stood up and made circular movements with his hands to keep up the children's noise level.

At the end of the beam Antonin jumped. He had never attacked a man in cold blood before, and he didn't want to have time to think about it.

He landed neatly on the sentry's back. The blow threw the sentry on to his face. The man opened his mouth to yell and Antonin stuffed hay into it. The man's machine gun was still slung across his back and Antonin was pulling at it to get it free. But he dared not let the man turn over. He punched him hard on the neck. He punched harder, holding his other hand round the man's throat, tilting the neck back.

The soldier had been stunned slightly by the fall and he was now recovering. His right hand began to creep forward as he hit out with his elbow to throw Antonin off his back.

The sentry was much bigger than Antonin, and Antonin knew he hadn't too long.

He caught hold of the sentry's elbow and tried to lock it in a half nelson, but the man let out a yell. Antonin punched him in the mouth. The man twisted and got his knee into Antonin's crutch. He felt a knuckle go into his eye. The sweat was pouring off his face and he was almost blinded by the injury to his eye. The man was now on his back and his hand had hold of the butt of the gun. He was trying to get his finger on the trigger.

Antonin felt his strength ebb away: Jesus I need help. Give me only one minute more.

He took a deep breath. The butt of the machine gun hit him in the chest. He was going. His head was swimming around in a

165

tank. He placed both hands on the man's waist. It was a matter of regaining his sight while he made one last lunge.

His left hand hit a knife. It was slung from the sentry's belt and its scabbard was fixed with a button. He flicked the button. The knife fell into his hand, ready for use. The sentry was searching with numbed fingers to flip off the safety catch on his machine gun.

Antonin plunged the knife into the man's chest with both his hands and he leant on it until the man stopped struggling. Then he took away his right hand and wiped the blood and sweat from his eyes.

The man was dead. His helmet was still rolling back and forth in a snow puddle. His right hand was on the machine gun trigger and the gun was pointed right at Antonin's chest. The sentry, when he looked closely at his face, was no older than Pavel.

48

When Antonin opened the door of the barn he was dressed in the uniform of an orderly of the German Corps of Engineers. His helmet sat over his eyes, his machine gun rested on his foot, his tunic was almost down to his knees and his trousers were baggy enough to fit two. He saluted in the Nazi fashion.

'So high!' he said.

The children broke into hysterical laughter. He quietened them. 'We're going to escape. There's no one outside right now and we can make our way across the meadow and into the trees. Once we're there they'll give us shelter in the farms of the village. But you must all be good and do as I say. We'll break up into three groups. That section there . . . ' he pointed to a group around Vera, 'will go with Miss Lydrakova. This section here with the doctor. The rest will come with me.' He paused. 'You must understand that this is a safety measure. If one group is spotted, the others must promise not to help them because they too will be killed. They must go ahead and make their own way to safety. Understand?'

The children nodded silently. 'Now, Miss Lydrakova's group . . . ' he was watching Samuel take hold of her hand, 'will go up the left side of the meadow. And they'll go first, keeping low through those tufts of grass. Then the doctor's group will go round the other side of the barn and start from there and work up the other end of the meadow.'

He paused again. 'Understand that too?'

There were grunts and nods.

'And my group. We'll start last and go through the middle of the meadow, keeping our arses down and crawling on hands and knees. But we'll not start until the other two groups have reached the shelter of the trees. Is that clear. Once we're in the trees we'll meet up again and make our way into hiding in the village.'

Every eye in the room was on him.

Vera came forward. 'If you are going to be a soldier, you might as well look more like one. You look like Charlie Chaplin.'

The children laughed and Vera straightened out the tunic.

'Tuck those trousers in more!' She pulled his belt round, 'Stick out your chest . . . no! *Chest*, not tummy!'

Within seconds Vera's party had started up the hill.

49

An ex-German General, a prisoner, raised a spade and brought it down on the neck of a German Corporal.

It was the beginning of a mass-scale and partly-organised revolt back at the train. The General then led several other prisoners in between two wagons, which they uncoupled. One wagon began to roll downhill to where a party of prisoners, Germans and people from the village were trying to take out the humped-up rails.

The General raised his arm, and waved his hand. Down at the working party the signal was acknowledged. The wagon gathered speed. A second before it was noticed a man from the village pushed a German soldier in the back with his spade. The two Germans working in between the rails didn't have a chance. The prisoners ran back and into the cover of the trees. Some stood in the trees to watch, others kept running.

The wagons collided with the humped rail and tipped over, careening down the bank and sending up puffs of snow.

Someone took the machine gun from the German caught under the rail and twisted it from his hand.

There was firing and shouting from the party up ahead of the train. About forty men, armed with picks and shovels, were coming down the line on the right hand side of the train. With them were a dozen or more newcomers, men from the village armed with hunting guns.

The party of fifteen men from the rear met with them and took cover behind the newly-overturned wagons. They had two stolen machine guns, four hunting rifles and some spades.

Under the General they formed a group of about eighty. The rest of the prisoners were running like rabbits. Some went into the wagons and sat and waited. Others made it to the railway platform.

The Germans were firing madly now. The SS document officer remained calm, his revolver drawn and under cover of a wheel behind what was left of the engine.

He was shouting orders to form up around him. But many of the Engineers had also climbed inside the wagons.

Up on the hillside, three hundred metres to the right of Antonin, an old woman had made the fence and was running for the group of trees at the top of the hill.

Quite suddenly there was a silence. The German General said, 'I need five volunteers to work their way with me down this side of the train and to take them in the rear from the hut by the platform.' He picked his men quickly and with care.

Crouched down, and with eyes fixed on the remainder of the engine, they padded forward in the soft snow.

50

Vera and her group were hiding half way up the meadow behind some clumps of grass. When they heard the firing it was impossible to stop the children from turning to see what was going on. So she made them all lie in the grass and wait. As soon as the shooting stopped she said, 'Come on now . . . all at once, and run like mad.'

The children got to their feet. Antonin saw them from the hut. He had just dispatched the doctor and his group up the left side of the meadow.

He noted with alarm that they were having a tough time slipping and sliding on the patches of iced snow. One boy, who was carrying a smaller boy on his back, was lagging behind.

He saw Vera turn and help drag the boy along. The first of Vera's party made the pines. The doctor's group started out.

A noise from down below, at the corner of the field, attracted Antonin's eye. Two soldiers, sent from the party which had formed round the officer, were running towards the meadow. The soldiers were calling for more men.

By now Vera and the last of her group had only yards to go. But the doctor was running in full view of the two soldiers.

They opened fire. There were perhaps fifteen in the doctor's group. They all hit the frozen grass hard. Antonin could see the doctor's bald head glinting in the sun.

He looked up the meadow and saw Vera running among the trees. He smiled and thanked God. The Germans were over the fence now and in the meadow. Antonin's reaction was to raise the machine gun which he had in his hands and fire at their crouching figures.

But he waited, fumbling with the safety catch. Suddenly the doctor's head popped up. What was he trying to do, the fool!

The head began to bob along in between the tufts of grass, making its way to the right. Suddenly his whole body was visible. The doctor was running in full view of the Germans.

When he was twenty paces from his hiding place, the boys and girls started out. They ran straight for the pines. Antonin counted heads. There were nine. The others must have been hit before they fell.

The Germans opened fire on the doctor. Antonin shouted, 'All of you start up the left side of the field. Heinrich and Jan, you stay with me. Go! Go I say!'

And almost with the same breath he shouted at the startled German soldiers who were only twenty metres to his right. Antonin pressed the trigger of his machine gun. Nothing happened. He banged it against his thigh. One German was aiming right at him now. From the corner of his left eye he saw the doctor plunge to the earth. He looked down at the gun. The safety catch was off and there was ammunition in it. His finger was gripping the trigger guard and not the trigger. The gun went off and the shots ricocheted off the logs of the barn.

The Germans were making for him now. Four of them. The other was running up the hill to where the doctor had plunged.

As he pulled Heinrich and Jan round the back of the barn, Antonin saw his party running up the hill towards the trees. If he could keep the Germans diverted for a few minutes they'd be safe.

He aimed the gun round the corner of the barn and pulled the trigger. The rebound nearly sent him to the ground.

The doctor was on his feet again. He appeared to have been hit in the shoulder. He was running from side to side, trying to make an angle so that his pursuer could not draw a bead.

Antonin never saw him make the pines, but he heard the cries of joy from somewhere inside that shelter. Vera had the children make a lot of noise. He supposed it was to take the heat off him.

'Heinrich and Jan . . . here, take this gun. Heinrich, can you? . . .'

'I can handle it, Mr Karas. Don't you worry. What are you going to do?'

'Take the gun and go round the other side of the barn. And make a run for it up the right side. You'll make it. Good luck. See you in the trees.'

The two boys started out. They were grinning. It was a game. A *real* game.

Antonin flattened himself on the ground and began to crawl up the hill towards where the doctor's group had first fallen. He was completely hidden for the first few metres. The soldier's uniform he was wearing was heavy and the buttons dragged in the snow and frozen grass. But he was glad he had it. It would help his last move. At a distance they wouldn't be able to tell. He tried to keep the helmet on the back of his neck, but the leather strap kept biting into his windpipe. He was determined nevertheless to keep it this way because he knew from his days in the theatre what an optical illusion such a thing can create at a distance.

He was humming to himself over those first few metres. He was enjoying the frozen ground being driven into his cut hands, the wet smell of the tunic cloth, even the pain of the cold in his ears. He was thinking of Vera there in the trees, running along safely with her brood of children, and of the love she felt for him. This is ridiculous, he said to himself, but I don't think I could make myself feel unhappy now even if I tried. He was proud of what he'd done too. Proud that he'd been able to keep his promise. The doctor would now be able to see that he was right. There always comes a time when it's your turn, when things go your way. He was a great man, the doctor, even though he was bossy and meticulous. He gave everything to those children.

Five metres to go, then he would wait a second and start the last stage. He could hear the Germans behind him whispering to each other as they searched the barn. He could hear their boots as they started out up the hill. He was not afraid. He knew what he was going to do. He was confident it would work.

Orchestra strike up the overture! Curtains ready. Lights. Curtains up! Here we go!

Antonin had the stage to himself and he was in command.

51

The pines smelled sweet. They were thickly planted, a reforestation project, and under them it was quite dark. Their boughs were laden with snow and apart from the occasional avalanche from the boughs there was complete silence.

Vera's first instinct was to take all the children and keep running. In fact she had started out. But the place was so dense that she could not be sure that she was going anywhere.

Then she'd been met by two women.

'We're from Glucholazy. Our men are down there fighting.'

'Can you help us find some shelter and food?'

'That's why they sent us. Everything is prepared.'

'Is it far?'

'About three kilometres. There is a place. The partisans are there. We've sent for them too. They'll soon finish off that fight.'

'The children are very tired and hungry.'

The older woman had no teeth. She was examining the faces and chewing on her gums. The younger one was excited, like a deer, running back and forth to make sure they were not being followed.

The doctor's group had arrived now and finally the doctor stumbled in holding his shoulder.

'It's only a graze. It's nothing. Let's go. Come on, we can't stop now. You boys carry the little ones.'

The young woman took the black scarf off her head and bandaged the doctor's shoulder.

He kept repeating, 'We must keep going. . . . Get moving will you . . . hurry! There's no time to be lost!'

He was herding all the children and dragging them like a madman through the pines.

Vera was tired, and she was nervous. She had never been so distracted in her life.

'Shut up!' she shouted, and she wanted to cry.

'What's the matter with you now?'

Vera stopped her tears.

'If it's Antonin and the other group you're worried about I'm staying here. We'll wait for them, but the rest must keep moving.'

'I'm staying. You go ahead,' said Vera.

'Don't let's stand here arguing, come along now . . . off with you. . . . Oh, very well then, you stay . . . I can't spend time arguing.'

Luckily at that moment, the first children from Antonin's group ran into cover.

'If you think we can waste time waiting, you're very much mistaken. It's our duty to get everyone away.' The doctor paused, 'There are six of my children lying dead in that field.' He left her.

'I'll wait here for the others. How many are there?' The young woman stopped her shepherding and came to Vera's side.

'A man, Mr Karas, Antonin Karas and perhaps two boys . . . he's dressed like a German soldier. . . . '

'You must not worry. He will be safe.' The young woman was looking at her intently. All the children were ahead now, silent under the doctor's orders and being led by the old tooth-less woman.

The young woman said, 'It really is better if you go ahead. They need you. Don't be upset. There is no firing. All that noise is down by the train.'

'When is Mr Karas coming?'

Vera swung round. It was Samuel.

'When is Mr Karas coming?'

'I don't know,' said Vera. 'But he'll be with us again soon. I'm sure. . . . '

The young woman bent down, 'Here, have some toffee?' Samuel shook his head. He was clutching the violin case. It was wet with snow, and one side had some grass sticking on to it.

'Yes, but *when* is he coming?'

Vera's nerves were going. She shut her eyes and said, 'All we know is that he's in the field and coming here soon, Samuel.'

'Why doesn't someone go to the edge of the trees and take a look for him. Maybe he needs help.'

'Oh shut up. For God's sake shut up!' Vera was trying to force back the tears.

'Why don't you go on,' the young woman had her hand on her arm. 'You are so tired and hungry. There's food and a bed and it's not a very long walk. I'll bring him to you. I promise you.'

Vera looked at the woman. The other party could barely be heard making its way, about half a kilometre ahead.

Suddenly she took hold of Samuel's arm. Her hand in his, she turned and started out up the path. It was better this way. If all was well and it would be, then the woman would bring him to her. If anything went wrong, then it was better to remember things . . . as they had been last night.

'Shall I take the violin?'

'No thank you!'

'Are you sure? It must be heavy.'

'I promised him I would not give it to anyone else.'

'All right, then you keep it,' she said. And they set off after the others.

52

The party working its way round the right side of the train, under the direction of the General, stopped.

The wagon ahead had had the side splintered and torn out by a bomb. The General pushed his head inside through the broken planking.

There were seventy or eighty people herded into the wagon. The General looked around. No soldiers.

'What the hell are you all doing here?'

The crowd saw his head for the first time and started to back away into the corner.

'You are free. Climb out this side! Hurry!'

They looked like lots of monkeys, old women and children with dark penetrating eyes, all staring at him.

'Com'n! Get out of there. You are free. Run for the woods. The people from the village will help you. We are all friends.'

But they only continued to press back into the corner.

The General was not a man to be diverted in his planning. He pulled his head out and gave the signal to creep forward.

Under the next wagon they caught the glimpse of a rifle barrel from behind a mound of earth thrown up by the first bomb. If only he had a grenade or a mortar. That'd get the bastard! Now they were all bastards, the Germans, and the common enemy of mankind – his own people.

There was spasmodic firing behind them. A few of the prisoners were taking pot shots at any movement on the platform.

The engine lay, a huge mass of twisted metal with dented wheels, about thirty metres ahead. It had been completely severed from its payload. There was a gap of seven metres in between. It was through this gap that the General was trying to lead his men. They were then to proceed to the northern end of the station.

The little wooden buildings, garnished with faded blue,

yellow and orange-flowered carpentry, could be seen plainly by the General from under the wagon now. The former customs shed at the northern end contained food and beer, a fact which the General had been transmitting to his men as an incentive all the way up the train. The General knew there was beer there, because when they had been led off the train yesterday, he had passed by as the Germans had forced the lock on the place.

But it was not for food and beer that the General wanted the shed. It was the highest vantage point in the station compound, and sooner or later more troops would appear coming down the road across the hill. Sooner or later another train would come. From the shed they could last out, provided they had the ammunition, for days against anything but heavy mortars and aircraft. The customs officers who had built the shed in the first place had not given themselves a clear view of the area for nothing.

The General's party was now poised at the gap. Seven metres. It seemed like more. Should take a man two seconds. Give him three. And send them over in pairs. If one gets hit, then he can drag the other.

The General raised his left hand and pointed two fingers in the air. The first pair set off. By luck and surprise they made the cover of the northern edge of the platform. The General could hear movement behind the engine. They'd seen his men and were repositioning a gun.

The next step was to make the three metres to the shed door. The General sent off his next pair. That left two behind, himself and a bull-necked Slovak named Juraj.

A sudden burst came from behind the engine. The two men rushing for the shed door were taken by surprise and fell dead, their arms stretched towards it.

The second pair made it. They even made it to the shed. The General was about to make the run himself when he first heard the car engines. He peeked over his shoulder and down the road.

A parade of armoured cars was coming up the hill, their camouflaged netting brushing the sides of the road and the hot scent of oil coming off their dulled paintwork.

The General didn't hesitate. 'Let's go,' he shouted.

Juraj got to the cover of the platform. The General fell a foot short of it. He could feel the hot bullets going into his flesh but he didn't care. He turned on his back and fired the machine gun at the open side of the overturned railway engine. He kept his finger on the trigger, the bullets pinging against the metal, until he fell dead.

53

During all the firing, Antonin had lain doggo. It had seemed to come from all around him and his followers were firing too. Antonin did not want to give his position away. He was hidden like a ferret between two mounds of earth, and although he couldn't see the enemy, he could hear him. What was important was that he could run from there to the pines in about fifteen seconds. That's all it would take.

Now that the firing had stopped he raised his body and started to run. Jan, on the other side of the meadow, saw him and started out too. Where the hell was Heinrich?

Jan was drawing fire from somewhere. Yes, by the barn. Antonin stood up fully. He turned to the Germans.

'You German bastards! You idiots. Look at those troops coming up behind you! You fools.' He was dancing about from leg to leg now and the Germans were coming out of the grass from all around him. Out of the corner of his eye he saw Jan slip into the woods.

'Why don't you fire at me! Look I'm not armed! Kill me! Are you afraid?'

Antonin stood still and calmly picked off a piece of dried grass. The Germans, there were five of them, were advancing slowly, their eyes on him and their guns ready.

'Want to take me alive?' he shouted. He was hoping that Heinrich would hear and make a run for it. But he saw no movement. Anyway, Heinrich was no doubt safe by now.

'Fire at me, you bleeding bastards,' he yelled.

But the Germans merely surrounded him and stood puffing, waiting for him to stop. Down by the station the armoured cars were disembowelling their troops. There was no rush.

Antonin was furious. But his anger was quick to disperse. It was replaced by irony.

He stood to attention. He faced his captors. He made the Nazi salute. 'That's how high my dog can jump,' he shouted.

They could not understand why he was laughing as they dragged him off. He only stopped when they passed over Heinrich's body, still clutching the gun in one hand, the other with his compass in it. Under express orders from the officer, who had been put in command of the prisoners, Antonin was to be kept in the custom shed until further orders arrived.

The pines were beginning to thin out. Patches of snow lay on the dead needles and crunched when you trod on them. The children were crying. Many of them were so tired that Vera thought they would never make another step. The doctor, despite his shoulder, had two on his back. She carried one. As did the old woman who was leading the way.

Ahead somewhere there was wood smoke.

'Want me to carry the violin for you now?' said Vera to Samuel.

'Where is he?'

'I should think he'll be here soon,' said Vera trying to smile.

'The lady up there told me it used to be a brigand's hut and we can all sit around in the middle of the house and eat until we can eat no more. What is venison? I think I shall like it better than beef. Mr Karas can play his violin. How far do you think it is now?'

'I think we're nearly there, Samuel.'

A gap in the forest lay ahead and a large log house stood in it. Outside, some men were cleaning guns and one man held a horse by the bridle. They ran forward and helped carry the children into the log house.

Vera had caught up with the old woman. She put down her child and sat on a stone.

She was absolutely exhausted. She began to cry.

The old woman put her arm round her, 'As long as you have life . . . why should you worry any more?'

The doctor, puffing and in pain, came to her.

'He'll be along. Just you wait!'

'They'll kill him. I know it.'

The doctor took Vera by the arm and led her into the warm hut. As she passed the door she heard Samuel say, 'He'll be here. He'll fool them. . . . He'll come, I've got his violin. . . . He's so funny.'

182

The snow had fallen heavily over Terezin. Its whiteness set in relief the greys and browns of the buildings. Early that morning, as Bürger stood at the phone in his office, the camp was aggravatingly still.

The officer from field headquarters on the other end of the phone was shouting the news of Antonin's capture and the restoration of order at the wrecked train. The message was being scrambled and unscrambled all the way, which probably accounted for Bürger's irritation. Words would drop away and the voice suddenly appear again like a jammed gramophone record.

The gist of what the fool of an Engineer Kommandant said was plain enough and Bürger knew it. When the man had finished he squeezed the phone hard into the palm of his hand and spoke in measured tones. The train was technically under his command until it reached its destination. And in any case one couldn't expect an officer of the Corps of Engineers to command. He was hardly qualified.

Bürger's hand relaxed and the colour came back to his knuckles wrapped round the phone. He replaced it on the silver hooks and sat down.

Outside he could hear orders being given for his tea.

'Perhaps I'm tired,' he thought, 'or perhaps that bloody engineer was more of a fool than I imagined.'

He looked up. His secretary was standing in front of him with a steaming cup of tea.

'Your tea, sir,' she said.

'I can see that, thank you.'

'Yes, sir. Hauptmann Läuffer is here with the Transport list. The Jewish Elders have. . . . '

'Transport list? . . . '

'For tomorrow's train.'

'Of course.' Bürger pulled himself to his feet and took a deep

183

breath. 'Tell him I'll look at it in the morning. How many children are on it?'

'Under thirteen, sir?'

'Yes, under thirteen!' Why was everyone being so stupid suddenly?

'I think the Hauptmann said three hundred, sir.'

'Very well, tell the Haptmann to work it all out with the Elders. I shall be in my house if anyone wants me.'

He walked to the door. 'How cold is it outside?'

'There's quite a wind, sir.'

His secretary was closing the door behind her.

Should he wear his heavy trench coat, or the field great coat? He stood looking at them for a second. Making the decision plagued him. He took first the trench coat and then replaced it.

'Aren't you going to drink your tea, sir?' It was his secretary again. At his side. He wondered if she'd seen him hesitate over the coat. 'Tea?' The steaming cup was still on his desk. 'Not today, thank you.'

Fifteen minutes later, while he was lying on his stomach in bed with his daughter's soft hands massaging his back and his face buried in the thick down of the pillow, he began to think again.

'You take everything too seriously, Papa!' she said. Her mouth was close to his ear.

He laughed into the pillow. It was impossible to see things out of perspective with her near him. He felt his body begin to relax.

'Soon the war will be over and you and I will take a long holiday . . . on the Mediterranean, perhaps?' She was laughing too, now. He turned over and held her shoulders.

They were both laughing. Although nothing was funny. It was a matter of release, he supposed. He kissed her lightly on the cheek and said, 'Yes, the Mediterranean.'

'It'll be the end of all that responsibility . . . and you can live a quiet normal life, drinking your English tea and taking the dogs for a walk along the beach. You can watch me while I swim.'

'Yes,' he said, but his thoughts were elsewhere. He was wondering, if it were all over . . . the war . . . the end . . . would it really be like that . . . or would it all live on?'

'Papa,' his daughter said, 'you're much too strong to let anything worry you for long, so don't worry. Besides, when you

wrinkle your eyes like that it makes you far too handsome!'
She returned his kiss lightly on the lips.

But Bürger's face remained closed to its thoughts. They
were closely and deeply imbedded like ivy already on the weak
walls of an old house.

The chaos and disruption around the station had been cleaned up. All the villagers found to have taken part in the rioting were shot and buried in a pit with the prisoners. Of the 3716 original prisoners on their way to Auschwitz, 2489 remained. The bodies of 864 killed in the bombing, or injured and now dead, had been buried in the huge pit. Three hundred and sixty-three were still missing. The armoured car Kommandant was sure that a search in the village and in the surrounding hills would make the totals tally exactly to the satisfaction of Leutnant Maler, the SS documentation officer. No one could survive a night at these temperatures in the woods, and without food prisoners would soon give themselves up.

The prisoners were herded into the thirty-eight wagons still on the rails in the front part of the train. The humped rail, like a twist in a piece of rubber band, refused to budge. The train-repair crew from Cracow would be here in the morning. That would give them time to round up the rest of the prisoners.

The armoured car Kommandant ordered food to be cooked for the prisoners, and set up toilets in the ditch to the west of the train.

The engine at the back of the train was in working order, according to the Engineers. And the three wagons attached to it, including 48, had survived.

The engine was now stoked and gathering steam. It would have to travel in reverse as far as Jesenik where there was a siding.

Antonin awoke suddenly. He had fallen asleep after being thrown into the customs shed. He hadn't wanted to go to sleep, but sleep had mercifully forced itself on him.

On one side of him were cans of meat, stacked in neat wooden boxes. Beef from the Argentine. On the other, in cardboard boxes, bottled beer.

Antonin rolled over. He tore open a carton and grabbed a bottle, smashing the top on the floor. He let it flow all over his face as well as in his mouth. It was cool and good. Three times he did this and when the door opened and two soldiers appeared, he was very drunk.

Behind the soldiers was the blurred form of the SS documentation officer.

They hoisted him up. He was singing and waving to the SS man.

It was almost dark outside. A pale ghost of a moon hung over the end of the train. And beside the tracks, where the men had been working, were the pot marks of now frozen boot imprints.

Antonin felt the tight grip of the soldiers under each arm. His feet were dragging as they marched. Behind, he heard the crunch of the SS man's boots.

They had reached the door of wagon 48 before the cold air brought him to his senses. The two soldiers were trying to lift him inside.

He turned and punched one of them in the stomach.

'What the hell d'you think you're doing? Where are you bastards taking me?'

He lashed out with his feet and all the fury he could summon.

One soldier was still doubled over. Antonin began to run down the track again. All he could see was Vera's face. He had no idea where he was running.

The two soldiers caught up with him quickly and dragged

him backwards, his legs kicking in the air like a child, to the door of the wagon.

The SS officer twisted his arm and he was flung inside the wagon.

'Shoot me! For Christ's sake shoot!' he screamed. 'I'm not a cow or a sheep!'

He began to lash out madly. 'Shoot me. I'll kill you.' He had his hands round the throat of the SS officer. A soldier raised his gun and took aim. The SS man pulled himself free and a punch landed Antonin on his back. 'I'll take on the lot of you . . . I don't care . . . I don't. . . .'

He flung himself at the three men again. The rifle was still aimed at his head. The soldier began to squeeze the trigger.

'Stop!' The SS officer knocked the rifle away. 'Beat him if you wish but he has to go on that train. Orders from my Kommandant.'

Antonin crawled to the door of the wagon again. 'Terezin? Is that it? You are sending me back?'

He raised his fist at the face of the officer. It carried with it all the comic training he had ever acquired. He brought the fist down with a crash. The officer ducked, but Antonin's left hand caught him in the mouth.

A soldier jumped up into the wagon and began to beat him on the head with his rifle butt.

'Leave him now. You'll kill him!'

'Please kill me. Please. I beg you. Kill me!' Antonin was sitting now, his legs crumpled under him and his swollen hands pleading. He grabbed the end of the soldier's rifle and put it to his head. The SS officer knocked it out of the way.

'Get out of the wagon. Just cover him and hit him if he moves.'

The officer was wiping his gloved hand over his bleeding mouth.

'We have something very special for you. I am not a sadistic man, and we will not kill you . . . you are to perform . . . to continue to perform . . . for the benefit of the Third Reich. Our glorious future . . . you will be contributing to it. It may even be put in history books . . . the clown who made children laugh . . . even as they were exterminated.'

Antonin wasn't listening. His brain was reeling. . . .

'There are orders to remove ten thousand more people from

Terezin this next month. Among them will be many children. . . . '

'I refuse . . . I will not do it!'

'You will. Is it not better to go to death with a laugh on your lips than in sadness?'

Antonin said quietly, 'You are . . . I can't understand! I simply can't understand!'

'There, it did not take too long to make you see sense? *Aufwiedersehen!* Goodbye my clown, and thank you!'

The door of the wagon jerked reluctantly shut. The bolts were put in place. A new chalk marking was placed upon the side and a padlock placed over the clasp.

Antonin was at first in complete darkness.

He stood a moment in silence, brushing down the soldier's tunic he still wore.

'I'm such a fool. People don't know what a fool I am!'

He kicked around in the straw as if he could find a thought in it which would lift him out of the dead end of his mind.

His foot hit the empty bucket. He kicked it. He kicked it again.

Then he stopped and picked it up. He tapped the bottom as if he were buying it and wanted to see if it were good.

He turned it upside down and stood on it. Before him suddenly was his audience. He could see them all, rows and rows of children. They were already laughing because he was performing automatically. He could smell the stale sausage, the garlic and the talcum powder. The dancers had been on before him. The audience seemed to go into the distance, fading into a mist, but up front were so many faces that would never leave him. They were crisply in focus and etched into his brain.

Antonin suddenly let forth a stream of language. It was German, yet it had no meaning . . . it was jibberish German. The audience was clapping and roaring. Some of the children were standing in their seats. He made the Nazi salute. No words came from his lips; but they laughed and laughed. . . .

The train jerked to a start. Antonin fell off the bucket. He picked himself up on his elbow. The audience had gone. He pulled the bucket underneath himself and sat with his chin cupped in his hands.

The train whistled. Its great wheels chugged downhill, back to where it had started.

It passed along, under the moon, and around the bend in the line.

The night was silent. It began to snow.

Gerry Moses's Farm,
Bolton, Ontario.

NEL BESTSELLERS

Crime

T013 332	CLOUDS OF WITNESS	*Dorothy L. Sayers* 40p
T016 307	THE UNPLEASANTNESS AT THE BELLONA CLUB	*Dorothy L. Sayers* 40p
T021 548	GAUDY NIGHT	*Dorothy L. Sayers* 40p
T026 698	THE NINE TAILORS	*Dorothy L. Sayers* 50p
T026 671	FIVE RED HERRINGS	*Dorothy L. Sayers* 50p
T015 556	MURDER MUST ADVERTISE	*Dorothy L. Sayers* 40p

Fiction

T018 520	HATTER'S CASTLE	*A. J. Cronin* 75p
T013 944	CRUSADER'S TOMB	*A. J. Cronin* 60p
T013 936	THE JUDAS TREE	*A. J. Cronin* 50p
T015 386	THE NORTHERN LIGHT	*A. J. Cronin* 50p
T026 213	THE CITADEL	*A. J. Cronin* 80p
T027 112	BEYOND THIS PLACE	*A. J. Cronin* 60p
T016 609	KEYS OF THE KINGDOM	*A. J. Cronin* 50p
T027 201	THE STARS LOOK DOWN	*A. J. Cronin* 90p
T018 539	A SONG OF SIXPENCE	*A. J. Cronin* 50p
T001 288	THE TROUBLE WITH LAZY ETHEL	*Ernest K. Gann* 30p
T003 922	IN THE COMPANY OF EAGLES	*Ernest K. Gann* 30p
T023 001	WILDERNESS BOY	*Stephen Harper* 30p
T017 524	MAGGIE D	*Adam Kennedy* 60p
T022 390	A HERO OF OUR TIME	*Mikhail Lermontov* 45p
T025 691	SIR, YOU BASTARD	*G. F. Newman* 40p
T022 536	THE HARRAD EXPERIMENT	*Robert H. Rimmer* 50p
T022 994	THE DREAM MERCHANTS	*Harold Robbins* 95p
T023 303	THE PIRATE	*Harold Robbins* 95p
T022 968	THE CARPETBAGGERS	*Harold Robbins* £1.00
T016 560	WHERE LOVE HAS GONE	*Harold Robbins* 75p
T023 958	THE ADVENTURERS	*Harold Robbins* £1.00
T025 241	THE INHERITORS	*Harold Robbins* 90p
T025 276	STILETTO	*Harold Robbins* 50p
T025 268	NEVER LEAVE ME	*Harold Robbins* 50p
T025 292	NEVER LOVE A STRANGER	*Harold Robbins* 90p
T022 226	A STONE FOR DANNY FISHER	*Harold Robbins* 80p
T025 284	79 PARK AVENUE	*Harold Robbins* 75p
T025 187	THE BETSY	*Harold Robbins* 80p
T020 894	RICH MAN, POOR MAN	*Irwin Shaw* 90p

Historical

T022 196	KNIGHT WITH ARMOUR	*Alfred Duggan* 50p
T022 250	THE LADY FOR RANSOM	*Alfred Duggan* 50p
T015 297	COUNT BOHEMOND	*Alfred Duggan* 50p
T017 958	FOUNDING FATHERS	*Alfred Duggan* 50p
T017 753	WINTER QUARTERS	*Alfred Duggan* 50p
T021 297	FAMILY FAVOURITES	*Alfred Duggan* 50p
T022 625	LEOPARDS AND LILIES	*Alfred Duggan* 60p
T019 624	THE LITTLE EMPERORS	*Alfred Duggan* 50p
T020 126	THREE'S COMPANY	*Alfred Duggan* 50p
T021 300	FOX 10: BOARDERS AWAY	*Adam Hardy* 35p

Science Fiction

T016 900	STRANGER IN A STRANGE LAND	*Robert Heinlein* 75p
T020 797	STAR BEAST	*Robert Heinlein* 35p
T017 451	I WILL FEAR NO EVIL	*Robert Heinlein* 80p
T026 817	THE HEAVEN MAKERS	*Frank Herbert* 35p
T027 279	DUNE	*Frank Herbert* 90p
T022 854	DUNE MESSIAH	*Frank Herbert* 60p
T023 974	THE GREEN BRAIN	*Frank Herbert* 35p
T012 859	QUEST FOR THE FUTURE	*A. E. Van Vogt* 35p

T015 270	THE WEAPON MAKERS	A. E. Van Vogt	30p
T023 265	EMPIRE OF THE ATOM	A. E. Van Vogt	40p
T017 354	THE FAR-OUT WORLDS OF		
	A. E. VAN VOGT	A. E. Van Vogt	40p

War

T027 066	COLDITZ: THE GERMAN STORY	Reinhold Eggers	50p
T009 890	THE K BOATS	Don Everett	30p
T020 854	THE GOOD SHEPHERD	C. S. Forester	35p
T012 999	P.Q. 17 – CONVOY TO HELL	Lund & Ludlam	30p
T026 299	TRAWLERS GO TO WAR	Lund & Ludlam	50p
T010 872	BLACK SATURDAY	Alexander McKee	30p
T020 495	ILLUSTRIOUS	Kenneth Poolman	40p
T018 032	ARK ROYAL	Kenneth Poolman	40p
T027 198	THE GREEN BERET	Hilary St George Saunders	50p
T027 171	THE RED BERET	Hilary St George Saunders	50p

Western

T016 994	EDGE No 1: THE LONER	George Gilman	30p
T024 040	EDGE No 2: TEN THOUSAND DOLLARS		
	AMERICAN	George Gilman	35p
T024 075	EDGE No 3: APACHE DEATH	George Gilman	35p
T024 032	EDGE No 4: KILLER'S BREED	George Gilman	35p
T023 990	EDGE No 5: BLOOD ON SILVER	George Gilman	35p
T020 002	EDGE No 14: THE BIG GOLD	George Gilman	30p

General

T017 400	CHOPPER	Peter Cave	30p
T022 838	MAMA	Peter Cave	35p
T021 009	SEX MANNERS FOR MEN	Robert Chartham	35p
T019 403	SEX MANNERS FOR ADVANCED LOVERS	Robert Chartham	30p
T023 206	THE BOOK OF LOVE	Dr David Delvin	90p
P002 368	AN ABZ OF LOVE	Inge & Stan Hegeler	75p
P011 402	A HAPPIER SEX LIFE	Dr Sha Kokken	70p
W24 79	AN ODOUR OF SANCTITY	Frank Yerby	50p
W28 24	THE FOXES OF HARROW	Frank Yerby	50p

Mad

S006 086	MADVERTISING		40p
S006 292	MORE SNAPPY ANSWERS TO STUPID QUESTIONS		40p
S006 425	VOODOO MAD		40p
S006 293	MAD POWER		40p
S006 291	HOPPING MAD		40p